MW01234320

SELVAGGIA STARK

"THE COTTAGE IN THE LEMON GARDEN"

"Loves Without Borders: Hearts on the Road.

Book 1"

I dedicate this work to all the people who have followed their hearts in life.

To all the people who still dream and want to make their dreams come true, even if it seems impossible.

I dedicate this story to my fellow travelers, to the people I have met and to those that the future will bring me. ....

To my first travel companion, my husband Giandomenico, who went to heaven too soon, to him I dedicate every breath and every beat of my heart....

To my twins who give me strength and life and to the good Lord who gave me the gift of writing.

And last but not least I dedicate all my stories to you, my readers.

Present and future, I think of you when I write to your faces, to your dreams....

Thank you

-SELVAGGIA STARK-

CHAPTER 1

I'm really tired, thought Emily as she attended the second meeting of the day.

Her head hurt.

She looked at the screen with the graphs and drawings and wondered if she could go on much longer.

She looked closely at her colleagues sitting at the meeting table and their faces were lifeless; for a moment she had the impression that she was not living, but surviving.

"How did I get here?" he asked himself as he looked out the large windows of one of the great skyscrapers that populate New York City.

"How did I forget who I am?"

"Mrs. Smith, what do you think about what your colleague Susan just said?" Emily looked at her boss, who was watching her from the back of the large conference table with the usual look of someone who wants to rip you off and make your life impossible.

At this question her colleagues turned in her direction and looked at her with that blank, submissive look they had always had stamped on their faces.

Emily suddenly heard a little voice inside him say, "Now I'm going to tell him to go to hell!!! Now is the time to do it! Emily rebel! It is time to change your life! No more getting up at the crack of dawn, taking the always crowded subway going to the cafe below the office and elbowing your way in to order a simple coffee'. No more!!! "

He glared at his boss and replied:

"Boss, I have no idea what my colleague Susan said, and I don't give a damn," then she calmly got up from her chair and walked over to her employer, who was looking at her with a look of surprise at her inappropriate behavior, and threw the reports she had written and spent several months preparing under his nose without ever receiving a thank you or an acknowledgement, let alone a promotion

Emily put her mouth close to the man's ear and whispered, "Do you know where you can put my reports?" At these words the man stood up and shouted, "Get out of my office, get out of my company. "Emily looked at him smiling and replied, "I will very gladly leave and tell all my colleagues who are watching me to wake up that there is only one life." And he turned and walked out of the room, slamming the door.

The secretary who was sitting outside at her desk next to the door of the meeting room heard the door slam and took off her glasses and looked at her with her usual squeamish look, Emily had put up with it for so many years she decided it was time she did the same.

"And you, Dorothy, I suggest you take that look off your big face because I'm in a bad mood today," the woman said as she got up and hid in the copy room. Emily laughed and happily made her way to her office, taking only her laptop, her parents' photo, and her coffee mug that her brother had given her.

She put everything in her bag and walked out, calling out to her colleagues who were working in the big hall with their greedy heads.

"I salute you, I, Emily, decided today to change my life. In fact, I decided to live." She took the elevator and left the skyscraper with satisfaction.

He began to walk and a happiness filled his heart. She felt light now that her new life was beginning.

Now the real Emily could truly call herself happy.

CHAPTER 2

He opened the door of his small apartment.

He was greeted by his little dog named Terry, who was wagging his tail and looking at him happily.

She came in, put her things on the small coffee table and threw herself on the couch, Terry immediately stood by her side and looked at her with a happy look..

"What do I do now?" Lying on the couch, she had her eyes fixed on the ceiling, "Of course, Emily, when you make them, you make them big," she whispered to Terry, who looked at her curiously. Of course she felt lighter now, without the nightmare of the job she had been doing for a long time, but what was she going to do now? She thought she was alone with a little dog. Her brother lived abroad and her parents traveled all year round, in fact they were supposed to be in some place' in India now and she?

"You know Terry, I think I made it big. I thought I was going to change my life, of course the thought of not going back to the office tomorrow makes me feel better, but now I'm out of work and have to pay a very expensive rent," after saying those words she looked around and thought, "Of course my landlord is such a thief ... when I think how much money I give him for this hole of an apartment," Terry suddenly got up from the couch, put the leash in his mouth and walked over to Emily. "Yeah, okay, let's go for a walk, maybe I'll get some ideas," and they went outside.

There was a park near his apartment where mothers with small children and dog owners hung out.

He walked into the park and immediately a friend of Terry's, a German Shepherd, walked up to him to say hello; the owner was a retired U.S. Army Lieutenant, a good friend of Emily's, and when he saw Terry barking and bothering his dog, he called out to him. "Bud, come on, leave Terry alone," he said in his typical big voice of someone who always gave orders in his life. Emily thought he was using a tone like he had to line up dozens of soldiers. Bud, his ears pricked up, ran obediently to his master and Emily walked up to him and greeted him, "Good afternoon, Tom, how are you?" The lieutenant quickly put the leash on Bud and replied, "Well, Emily, I am feeling good today, some of my wife's relatives came to visit us and when they come they always give me cheer! They are very sunny and nice people, and they brought lots of delicious food," Emily asked curiously, "Where are they from?" Tom smiled and replied, "From Italy," Emily smiled and said, "How nice Italy, I love Italy, I love Italian movies, fashion and cooking, and let's not talk about the language, a few months ago I took an online Italian course, it wasn't easy, but now I speak a little Italian too.

There was a park near his apartment where mothers with small children and dog owners hung out.

He walked into the park and immediately a friend of Terry's, a German Shepherd, came up to him to say hello; the owner was a retired U.S. Army Lieutenant, a good friend of Emily's, and when he saw Terry barking and bothering his dog, he called to him. "Bud, come on, leave Terry alone," he said in his typical big voice of someone who always gave orders in his life. Emily thought he used a tone that made it sound like he had to line up dozens of soldiers. Bud, his ears pricked up, ran obediently to his master, and Emily walked up to him and greeted him, "Good afternoon, Tom, how are you?" The lieutenant quickly put the leash on Bud and replied, "Well, Emily, I am feeling good today, some of my wife's relatives came to visit us and when they come they always give me cheer! They are very sunny and nice people, and they brought lots of delicious food," Emily asked curiously, "Where are they from?" Tom smiled and replied, "From Italy," Emily smiled and said, "How beautiful Italy, I love Italy, I love Italian movies, fashion and cooking, and let's not talk about the language, a few months ago I took an online Italian course, it wasn't easy, but now I speak a little Italian too.

Tom continued, "My wife's cousin and his wife own a restaurant on the island of Capri, my wife and I went there a few years ago and I must say it is a real paradise.

The sea, the sun, the lemon trees, the flowers all year round, the mild climate, it really is a spectacular island, we would love to go back there," he said as he looked around with a sad look at the tall skyscrapers around them and the gray sky, shrugging his shoulders, he said in a sad voice, "Instead we are here with this climate and this sky," they both looked into each other's eyes and remained silent. Emily then, to change the subject, told the Lieutenant what had happened in the office and that she had decided to quit her job. He listened to her carefully and then said with a strong voice, "You did well, Emily, I am happy for you, you were brave. And she gave him her hand in congratulation.

Tom saw a worried face on the girl's face after his words and asked him, "Looking at you, I get the feeling that you are not convinced of what you did this morning. Why is that?"

Emily looked at him and answered honestly, "What do I do now?" Tom patted him hard on the shoulder and said, "Real soldiers do not abandon the field, they keep fighting even when the enemy is close, and so must you. Don't give up!!!" Then he suddenly asked him, "Listen, if I invite you to dinner, will you come? That way you will finally meet my wife and her Italian relatives, what do you say? It seemed like a good idea to Emily, she needed to have nice and cheerful people around her, so she replied, "All right, I'll be very happy to come," Tom said happily, "Well then, I'll expect you at seven o'clock," and waving goodbye, he 'left' with his German shepherd.

Emily looked at him as he walked briskly away from her and thought, "Well, actually, we are at war. I must defend myself against the enemies. And she walked on, thinking of the different solutions she could undertake.

CHAPTER 3

She arrived on time for her appointment; she had bought a beautiful bouquet of flowers to give to the hostess.

Tom opened the door and greeted her with a big smile, "Come Emily, have a seat!" As soon as she entered the apartment she was flooded with delicious smells, she turned in the direction where the smells were coming from and saw the kitchen full of people talking loudly and moving around the stove, they were cooking gesticulating and some were singing. Emily stopped to watch them, Tom saw her enchanted expression and said to her, "What did I tell you? They bring cheer to the house, the sun and the sea," then he took her under his arm and gently led her into the kitchen to introduce her.

When she entered, she was overwhelmed by the smells and the countless dishes on the kitchen peninsula. Tom raised his voice and said, "Dear friends, may I present Emily, our guest for tonight!!!"

Everyone fell silent and looked at her, realizing what Tom had said, she was bathed in handshakes, caresses and compliments. Emily stood there smiling at the people talking to him, holding the bouquet in her hand to keep it still, then finally a voice interrupted the chaos. "Please be quiet! "

A woman in a white apron approached Emily "Excuse me but we Italians are like that, we are warm and we like physical contact even just to say hello " then taking the bouquet of roses she said "Hello Emily I am Maria the wife of Tom" admired the flowers and thanked her . Emily with her eyes still dazed by that warm welcome only managed to say "You're welcome " . Tom picked her up and led her into the hall. There was a large table set for ten people .

little later a man with a dark mustache and thick hair, dressed in a white suit and a flower in his buttonhole, a red rose, came out of a room adjacent to the hall.

Tom and the girl sat down on the couch while the chatter had resumed from the kitchen "Let me introduce myself I am Gaetano, Maria's cousin and owner of the most 'beautiful restaurant in Capri," he smugly admitted, shaking Emily's hand.

Now she sat between Tom and Gaetano, who had a habit of smoothing his moustache when he thought.

Emily looked out the window and saw that Tom had a beautiful lemon plant on the balcony; it was covered with plastic to protect it from the cold.

Emily liked lemons, it was a fruit she used a lot in the dishes she prepared, she loved the sour taste and sometimes when the lemons were unprocessed she could even taste the peel.

"It's ready!" called Mary as she came out of the kitchen, the other women behind her in single file, each carrying a different dish. In no time the table was filled with innumerable dishes, overflowing with food that Emily's eyes were filled with wonder as she exclaimed. How wonderful it is to see," she took her cell phone out of her pocket and asked for permission to take some pictures, she'd post them on her Instagram profile, sure to get a lot of likes. The cooks, proud of their work, posed and Emily took a few photos of them as well, as souvenirs.

Then everyone sat down contentedly.

Emily was surprised that there were really ten people at the table, everyone began to speak in Italian, happily passing the large colorful plates full of food among themselves.

Tom helped her explain what it was all about as dishes came to her" This Emily is a parmigiana made with eggplant. I recommend it, it is excellent.

Then here is spaghetti with clams, you have to try that, and over there, as you can see, are hors d'oeuvres with some cold cuts that come directly from Italy.

Emily felt like she was in culinary heaven, the colors and smells emanating from these dishes were extraordinary. She closed her eyes and felt as if she had been catapulted to Italy.

Gaetano poured her a glass of red wine and confessed that it was an Italian wine brought directly from the island of Capri by a friend of his.

The man then pointed to his wife and called her "Rosa! Pass Emily the bread you made this morning" Rosa a middle-aged lady with dark hair and blue eyes smilingly handed him slices of a homemade bread that was arranged in the middle of the table.

The man took the slice and immediately put some olive oil and anchovies and a slice of good ham on it, then he gave it to Emily, she opened her mouth and took the first bite, at that moment a myriad of flavors filled her mouth, she was immersed in a world of tastes she never imagined existed.

The people at the table stopped talking and turned to her to see the reaction of an American girl tasting the products of their land that they called "Heavenly Nectars".

Emily closed her eyes and quietly enjoyed the bite, then opened them again to see those faces watching her, waiting for her word or comment. Smiling, she could only utter, "Unbelievable, fantastic," satisfied, they smiled and resumed their conversation.

"What do you do in life, Emily?" Asked Gaetano who was sitting next to him, Emily continued to eat with gusto and replied "Well nothing, I just quit my job" the man opened his eyes wide in amazement "Fired and why?" she finished the bite and took a sip of the excellent wine she replied "I got tired of working in a place where you are not respected and they steal your time to live" Gaetano smiled and patted the girl on the shoulder and replied happily "Bravo . .We Italians don't live to work but we work to live" and raising his glass he called out loud "Let's drink to Emily and her new life" everyone raised their glasses and shouted "To Emily".

In addition to Tom, his wife, and Gaetano and Rosa, other Italians who had lived in New York for many years, Italians who had businesses such as restaurants and shops of various kinds, were invited.

Emily was fascinated by these people, especially Gaetano, who immediately seemed to be a friendly and very nice person. Tom watched her eat and was pleasantly surprised at how quickly she made friends with all these new people. He thought he was discovering a new side to his friend whom he met every morning at the park, a friendship that began when his dog, Bud, befriended her puppy, Terry, one day. The man immediately thought she was a good girl, but from her behavior and the way she talked about her work, he got the impression that she did not feel fulfilled, that she had a burden, something in her heart that did not make her feel good about herself and others.

Sometimes, when I saw her walking with a frown or a worried look on her face, lost in thought, holding her cell phone, which she looked at countless times while walking her dog, she seemed obsessed with her work.

Now, however, on this day, around this table full of joy and happiness, her face had changed expression, her eyes shone and had a new light, her formerly serious mouth was now smiling and happy.

Dessert came, but Emily felt full. Rosa handed her the plate with a slice of cake and said, "Emily, you can't miss the famous Pastiera Napoletana, a traditional Neapolitan dessert," the girl, admiring the slice on the plate, couldn't resist and tasted this fantastic dessert as well.

When dinner was over, the women took the dishes off the table, Emily offered to help, and then sat down on the couch. Gaetano drank his coffee, looked at Emily and asked, "Emily, would you like to come work in my restaurant? I need an American to help me with all my foreign customers who stay and come to my restaurant. Would you help me, what do you think?" Emily stood there looking at him in disbelief at the suggestion she had just heard and at that moment in her mind she imagined the sea, the sun, the beaches and the good food caught up in the excitement she answered without hesitation and without thinking twice "Yes! I will come very willingly". Gaetano, seeing her face so determined and determined, smiled and said, "Well done Emily, I understood that you are a determined girl, as for the accommodation, do not worry, we have a small apartment above the restaurant, you would not spend anything".

Emily smiled, she was happy. YES!!! It was time to turn the page in the book of her life.

Gaetano stood up from his chair and shook Emily's hand, "Well, I'll be expecting you in a few weeks. Just bring your little dog, a suitcase and your beautiful smile, the rest is up to us."

Emily, in an impulsive gesture, hugged Gaetano and jumped for joy, shouting, "Italy, I'm coming!!!"

Out of the kitchen came the women with frightened faces to see what was happening in the room they had heard shouting, the scene they saw was that of Emily happily embracing Gaetano and Tom .

CHAPTER 4

"Hi Sarah, I have some great news for you," Emily said with excitement in her voice.

She was sitting in her favorite bar with her best friend, it was cold outside, it was spring but the weather had no intention of changing, it had been several days since rain flooded the streets of New York.

Sarah stared at her intensely; the last time she had heard from her was the day her friend had quit her job. There had been only a few phone calls since then, but now they had finally found the time to see each other. Emily had mentioned something about an important decision she wanted to tell her.

Knowing her friend to be a person of unexpected and sudden decisions, Sarah was a little worried, in fact, she was sitting next to her eagerly waiting for her to reveal her important news.

"I've decided to move to Capri, Italy!"

Sarah was speechless for a moment, but then exclaimed, "Oh my God, Emily, this is incredible news! But what made you make this decision so suddenly?"

Emily smiled, feeling her friend's excitement. "You see, I have been wanting a change in my life for a long time. I have always loved Italy and everything it has to offer. So I decided it was time to follow my heart and start a new adventure. "She then told about meeting Tom and having dinner at his house and about Gaetano's offer.

Sarah listened excitedly, it was amazing that so much had happened in such a short time, she was happy for her friend.

After breaking up with her boyfriend, Emily had become withdrawn, rarely going out with her and her friends; she had become very pessimistic about life and her future.

When she got the news that she was going to quit her job, on the one hand, she was happy because she knew that it was not a job for her to stay in the office all day, writing reports for a software company.

Emily was a girl of charming figure and medium height. Her slender figure enhanced her innate elegance. Her dark, long, wavy hair framed large black eyes like two sparkling gems that shone with a rare intensity and captured the attention of anyone who met her gaze. Her thick eyebrows added depth to her gaze, giving her a unique and penetrating expression. But what was most striking about Emily was her smile-a beautiful smile that lit up her face, a smile that could melt ice and warm hearts. Without a doubt, Emily was a person of extraordinary beauty.

A woman of eclectic style. She loved to dress elegantly with an eye for detail. Her satchels were an essential accessory in her wardrobe, carefully chosen to complete her outfits.

Despite her love of elegance, Emily did not sacrifice comfort when it came to running. She wore colorful tracksuits that reflected her energetic personality. Orange and pink was one of her favorites, a bold combination that reflected her passion for life.

Whether it was a formal event or a run in the park, Emily knew how to dress for the occasion, proving that style and function can go hand in hand. Her attention to detail and ability to mix and match colors made her an all-around style icon. Emily was a perfect example of how to be both stylish and practical.

In addition to her passion for running, Emily had a passion for writing, she had started to write a novel, but unfortunately, although several months had passed, she still had not finished it. Sarah had been the only one lucky enough to read a few pages and she was thrilled, it was really good, of course the story had stopped halfway through but she believed that one day it would be a success if she committed to finishing it.

Now that she saw her friend so enthusiastic, she thought that in Italy, with the sun and the sea and the peace that she had not found in New York, she could finish it.

Sarah was the epitome of the classic American girl. With her blonde hair, with a somewhat fleshy figure, she had a charm all of her own, from the big blue eyes that gave her a sweet look, although of great strength and personality, she possessed a gift of empathy that had always helped her since childhood, she could recognize people at first glance and was rarely wrong. She worked for a marketing firm in New York.

Despite her penchant for casual wear, Sarah had a soft spot for fashion, especially Italian fashion.

She loved simplicity and comfort, but never sacrificed style. Her sartorial choices reflected her personality: laid-back but fashion-conscious. She often wore comfortable jeans, oversized t-shirts and stylish sneakers. But what made her style unique were her accessories: colorful bracelets, hoop earrings and, of course, an always fashionable satchel.

Despite her casual style, Sarah had an eye for high quality fashion. She loved great Italian designers, and if she could save some money, she would not hesitate to buy a high fashion accessory or dress. This mix made her style unique and distinctive.
Ultimately, Sarah was a girl who knew how to be herself through her style, how to mix casual with elegant, comfort with fashion, and create a look that was all her own. Sarah was proof that you can be fashionable without sacrificing comfort and practicality.

The still incredulous girl asked, "But what about your little apartment here in New York?" she asked worriedly.

Emily sighed slightly. "Well, I must confess that I am happy not to be throwing away so much money on that small and uncomfortable accommodation, I am sure I will not miss it. The Isle of Capri offers me the chance to radically change my existence, with a different culture and its thousand-year-old traditions, and then being near the sea, it has always been my refuge."

Sarah asked enthusiastically, "When are you leaving?"

Emily ordered another beer and said, "A week."

Sarah blinked and shouted, "A week," people in the bar turned to look at her curiously, she turned red with embarrassment, lowered her voice and demanded, "What? A week?"

"Yes Sarah, at the restaurant they need me, Gaetano called me the other night and informed me that many Americans are coming, you know spring is the favorite time for tourists because of the mild weather.

As for the apartment, I called the landlord and he told me not to worry because he has his nephew who is planning to move to New York to study..." and with a beaming face he raised his glass and said "Let's toast to the new Emily and my new life" Sarah, still stunned by the news and the impending departure, also took her glass and toasted with her best friend who was leaving for Italy.

Sarah approached Emily and gave her a warm hug. "I am so proud of you for making such a brave decision! I know you will be successful in this new adventure. And you know what? Everyone will be so lucky to have you in Capri!"

Emily felt encouraged by Sarah's words. "Thank you, Sarah. It means a lot to me to know that you have my back. I want to ask you a favor. Could you take care of Terry until I get settled? You will bring her to me when you join me.

Sarah smiled and nodded. "Absolutely, you don't have to worry, Terry and I get along just fine, and then it will be an excuse to come to you as soon as possible! I look forward to visiting Capri and spending time with you on that beautiful island. I hope this new chapter in your life brings you happiness and fulfillment.

The two friends hugged again, knowing that despite the distance, their friendship would remain strong and Emily would begin a new, unforgettable adventure in Capri!

CHAPTER 5

Emily arrived on Capri on a beautiful spring day. The sun shone high in the sky without a cloud, and the weather was pleasantly mild. With a little apprehension and a little excitement, she boarded the boat to the enchanting island of Capri. Her excitement grew as the ferry approached the harbor

She had waited a long time for this day; she was excited about her new beginning in a foreign land and a new language that she had recently learned to speak. The sun shone brightly in the blue sky, illuminating the crystal clear sea that surrounded the boat.

Feeling the salty breeze on her skin, Emily allowed herself to be enveloped by a sense of freedom. She gazed at the breathtaking panorama unfolding before her: rocky coastlines, hidden caves, and villas surrounded by lush greenery. The colorful traditional houses clung to the shore, overlooking the deep blue sea. She was already in love with this island.

Emily entered the restaurant and was immediately enveloped by the irresistible aromas of Italian cuisine. The sound of the lively conversation of the customers filled the place, while the tables were carefully set with light blue tablecloths.

The nautical-style restaurant was a charming place that made you feel like you were in a typical fisherman's tavern. In a tranquil atmosphere surrounded by Mediterranean nature, it offered a breathtaking view of the crystal clear sea stretching to the horizon.

Its elevated location allowed every table to enjoy a spectacular panoramic view, creating a romantic and relaxing atmosphere. The walls of the restaurant were decorated with paintings of seascapes, sailboats and colorful fish, adding a touch of authenticity. The tables were set with blue and white striped tablecloths that resembled the sails of a boat. Light wood furniture evoked the rustic charm of typical fishing boats. The restaurant's menu offered a wide selection of fresh seafood dishes and seafood specialties. Seafood hors d'oeuvres, aromatic fish soups and first courses such as spaghetti with clams and sea urchin were some of the delicacies to be enjoyed. Like the first courses. Ravioli capresi, a dish that is always present on the menus of the restaurants of Capri. They are ravioli stuffed with cheese (mainly caciotta) and marjoram, served with sauce and basil. The famous Caprese salad, which Emily loved and enjoyed sometimes even in New York, consists of mozzarella, tomatoes, basil and oil: simple, very tasty and typically Caprese.

Main courses included mixed grilled fish, seafood chowders and tasty fish with a side of fresh vegetables.

The cozy atmosphere, the exquisite food, the spectacular view of the sea and the courtesy of the staff made Gaetano and Rosa's restaurant in Capri an unforgettable place for a first-class seafood experience.

Rosa, the owner, saw her enter and approached her with a warm smile.

"Welcome to Capri, Emily!" said the woman enthusiastically. "We are happy you have arrived and have been waiting for you."

Emily smiled, immediately feeling at ease. She looked around and saw Gaetano, the cook, behind the stove, whose kind face waved at her.

"You'll learn a lot from Gaetano," Rosa continued. "You'll be working side by side with our boys, who will help you settle in."

Emily was filled with gratitude for the warm welcome. She felt that this place would become a landmark for her, a place where she would make precious memories and learn so much about the food and culture of the island.

Rosa took her by the hand and asked her to follow, with her backpack Emily followed, they took a staircase outside the restaurant that led to the second floor where her apartment was located.

Rosa took out the key she had in her pocket and gave it to Emily, saying with a sweet smile, "You open it! Emily excitedly took the key with the anchor shaped key ring and opened the door.

The apartment was decorated in a nautical style, with light and fresh colors, reminiscent of the sea and sand. The walls were painted white and a delicate blue, while the floors were made of light wood.

The furniture was made of rattan to evoke the natural elements of the beach. An armchair in the middle of the room was upholstered in cotton fabric with blue and white stripes.

In each corner of the room were white wooden tables, on each of which were nautical-style lanterns, coral, shells were collected in a wicker basket on the table next to the kitchen.

A few paintings of seascapes, nautical maps and photographs of boats hung on the walls.

Emily was speechless, it was a beautiful apartment, upon entering she had the impression of stepping into a cabin on a ship.

She turned to herself and could only say, "Rosa is wonderful," the woman, happy that she appreciated the apartment, motioned for her to follow her into the bedroom.

A double bed with a white wooden headboard on which rested a necklace of white shells, next to the bed was a small table with a lamp also made of wood but blue in color, the closet was white, but what left Emily speechless was the small window from which one could admire a breathtaking spectacle, the entire gulf was visible from there Emily turned to Rosa who understood her thoughts and said, "Emily, from here you can see the majesty of the island".

Under the window was a small desk and a wooden chair, also blue.

A small bathroom off the bedroom contained a bathtub, and above the white sink was a white, wood-framed mirror with nautical details reminiscent of those found in ship's cabins.

Emily then walked with Rosa to the small kitchenette, which had two burners, a small refrigerator, and a peninsula where she could work or have breakfast in the morning. There were colorful cups and pots and pans in a small cabinet, also made of white wood, along with cutlery and other kitchen utensils. Rosa opened the doors for the girl to see, then satisfied, she said goodbye to Emily and waved, "Take your time unpacking your backpack, then if you want to come to the restaurant," and closed the door quietly.

Emily left alone, removed the backpack she still had on her shoulders, and took another tour of the house. It was truly a dream, unlike the apartment she had in New York, she went to her bedroom and opened her closet, putting her things down, then lay down on the bed.

A light breeze came in through the small window, the air gently moving the thin white curtains, Emily watched the movement and smiled happily, then tiredly closed her eyes and fell asleep.

CHAPTER 6

The sound of someone knocking on the door woke Emily, who opened her eyes and only remembered after a few seconds that she was on a Mediterranean island.

She struggled to her feet and began to open the door.

In front of her stood Gaetano looking at her curiously, he smiled at her and said, "Emily, it's morning, you've slept for almost a day now, it's time to get to know the island, tonight I need you. They have a large group of Americans booked. So come on, be brave, I'll wait for you at the restaurant so you can have a nice breakfast and we'll get organized. After saying these words in a rather high tone, he patted the poor girl's still sleeping shoulder.

He left Emily, closed the door and looked at the clock, it was 9 a.m. He had actually slept a lot.

He went to the bathroom and freshened up, then dressed in white.

Bermuda shorts and a blue shirt with sneakers and walked down to the restaurant.

Entering through the back door was the working girl, deftly moving among the tables, setting and arranging cutlery and glasses...she wore a uniform that consisted of a light blue dungaree-like apron with a belt, also light blue, where utensils that could be used to open bottles and other things hung, and a pocket to hold orders and a pen.

The girl saw her enter and greeted her with a smile.

"Come on Emily, I'll buy you a nice cup of coffee," Gaetano called from the kitchen, and Emily ran into the kitchen.

On the center table were wooden crates with the freshest fruits and vegetables, basil, sage and rosemary were in a large glass jar placed near the fireplace.

The kitchen where Gaetano worked was a sight to behold. Hanging on the walls, the shiny copper of the pots and pans gleamed in the sunlight streaming in through the large glass window. Each pot was perfectly in place, creating an atmosphere of order and precision.

Over the fire, large pots simmered with irresistible aromas, emitting fragrances that wafted throughout the kitchen. Gaetano, with mastery and concentration, mixed ingredients with innate skill, creating traditional recipes and gourmet dishes.

In one corner of the kitchen were several boxes of fresh fish, freshly caught in the Sea of Capri. The catch was ready to be cleaned and cooked. Emily, a young apprentice, watched with rapt eyes, eager to learn from Gaetano every secret of his culinary art.

The smell of the food being prepared mingled with the heat of the flames and the sound of knives cutting and chopping ingredients. The kitchen was full of movement and life as Gaetano moved with grace and speed, working harmoniously to create gastronomic works of art that would satisfy the desires of the restaurant's customers.

As she watched Gaetano grapple with the culinary creations, Emily realized how lucky she was to have the opportunity to learn and work in such a fascinating and inspiring restaurant and kitchen. She thought that this restaurant in Capri was a magical place, where passion for food and culinary artistry merged into one extraordinary experience.

Emily enthusiastically admired everything around her, the kitchen was a colorful and lively place there were many tomatoes scattered on the table ready to be cooked and make fresh sauces, red, green and yellow colored hot peppers hanging on the wall near the fires ,hand painted ceramic containers filled with spice plants .

Gaetano stepped away from the counter and grabbed a cup and poured him some coffee from the large mocha, then he opened the oven and grabbed a small puff pastry and gave it to Emily, she took the plate and cup and sat down shyly in the corner of the kitchen, took a sip of this 'excellent coffee with a strong flavor then took a bite of the mini puff pastry and cream pie...incredibly good and she was already feeling better as she enjoyed her first real Italian breakfast.

He watched with the wonder and curiosity of a child full of amazement, enthusiasm and eagerness to learn.

His parents had been overjoyed to learn the news of his departure; they, too, loved Italy. They had visited it on their honeymoon, and they had fallen in love with it. Over the years they had vowed to return there, but unfortunately, because of her father's job as a teacher in a private school, they had been unable to return.

Sure enough, the girl thought that one day she would see them suddenly arrive with their suitcases to spend some time with her and visit the island.

"Emily, are you ready?" asked Rosa as she entered the kitchen, and the girl, quickly getting off the stool, replied, "Yes. I feel strong and fit after your Italian coffee.

Emily was excited to work in such a fascinating environment and to start her first day of work. Rosa took her on a quick tour of the restaurant and introduced her to the staff. The woman explained her duties as a waitress, which included taking orders, serving customers, and keeping her own assigned tables clean, as well as helping in the kitchen when needed.

The girl was determined to do a good job. She began to learn the menu and memorize the restaurant's specialties. She vowed to always be attentive to customers' needs and to provide friendly and professional service.

"Emily, will you come with me?" asked Gaetano, the girl joined him and they went out the back of the restaurant and he saw a small vintage Ape Fiat passenger car, consisting of only two seats in the front while the back was open with three wheels. "Come with me, I want you to meet our fruit seller," and he made her get in the front seat next to him. The car was very small, barely fitting two people, the man laughed and drove off

It was a sunny morning, and Gaetano decided to let Emily explore the enchanting island of Capri before they reached the greengrocer's. The man drove nimbly in the little red car that seemed to have lost none of its charm over the years.

The radio was on, playing Italian tunes, and the two began their journey through the picturesque winding streets of the island. Their faces were lit by the contagious smiles between them as the sea breeze brushed their cheeks.

The narrow cobblestone streets were awash with bouquets of colorful flowers decorating the windows of Capri's cozy homes. The scent of sweet oranges and juicy lemons wafted through the air and into the interior of the car as the two smiled and breathed in the fresh, invigorating aroma.

Gaetano deftly maneuvered the steering wheel as Emily gazed in fascination at the panorama that opened up before them. The island of Capri offered a breathtaking view of the crystal clear sea and sheer cliffs, creating a magical backdrop.

Gaetano slowly approached the greengrocer. Emily got out of the car, her hair tousled by the wind and a beaming smile on her face, as Gaetano joined her and they walked together toward the fruit store. The owner, an elderly gentleman named Beppe, wearing a straw hat and apron, greeted Gaetano with a friendly attitude, the man introduced Emily, "Beppe, this is Emily, the new girl working with us at the restaurant, she is American" Beppe smiled at her and took off his hat, made a little bow of greeting and said to her, "Good morning young lady, I am Beppe at your service" then he took a beautiful orange from a wooden box he had next to him and placed it there, Emily accepted the fruit and smelled the scent it gave off, it was very strong, She opened it and it was incredibly juicy and of a strong orange color," the two men smiled as they saw how energetically she tasted the orange and Beppe said happily, "Our oranges are the best," Gaetano went off to carefully examine the fresh fruit, oranges, lemons and melons, looking for the perfect ones for the restaurant, then on Beppe's instruction, Gaetano went to the vegetables, salads, potatoes, zucchini and some beautiful bunches of zucchini flowers, Beppe observed the expression of wonder on the girl's face, who admired with amazement all those beautiful vegetables and said: "The vegetables come directly from my garden, with this sun and this sea air the vegetables grow twice as big as those found in big cities".

The caterer took a lot of fruits and vegetables and then, after loading the bee, greeted the greengrocer who returned the greeting with a small bow and gave another orange to Emily, whispering, "For the journey".

Satisfied, Gaetano and Emily returned to the restaurant, the chef told them about Beppe and confided, "Beppe is a man from another time, he has traveled a lot, he has been to many parts of the world, America, Thailand, and Greece, but then he came back home. The land where he is building the greenhouse and the large vegetable garden has been in his family for generations, all the restaurants get their supplies from him because they are sure of his honesty and care for his produce" Suddenly from the radio came a song that

Emily knew, "O Sole Mio," Gaetano happily turned up the volume and began to sing it at the top of his voice.

To Emily at that moment, with the sun high and its rays so bright, the car speeding along those narrow streets overhanging the turquoise-colored sea, the scent of aromas in the air, it seemed to her that she was living in a dream.

As they drove back through the same picturesque roads they had used on their way out, their faces reflected in the windshield were full of satisfaction and happiness. There was something magical about that moment, in the combination of the island of Capri and Gaetano's passion for his land, his music and even his work, which made those moments unique and magical for Emily.

The man, unaware of Emily's presence, sang impetuously and passionately; Emily looked at him and thought it was nice to have this spontaneous and impulsive character, and was a little envious of him.

They arrived at the restaurant.

Emily was still holding the orange Beppe had given her, she would eat it later, now she had to start working, the customers would be arriving soon.

Gaetano brought everything into the large kitchen, then put on his chef's apron and began to prepare the menu.

Emily, called by Rosa, helped her prepare the tables.

Then they went with her to the large garden that adjoined the restaurant and where her house stood.

The garden near Rosa's restaurant was a botanical paradise, enhanced by flowers that grew in abundance on the island of Capri. The women were greeted by an explosion of colors and delicate scents as they passed through the garden gate.

An enchanting spectacle presented itself to his eyes, a variety of flowers following one another in perfect harmony. Among the most common plants were beautiful bougainvilleas with their purple, yellow, and fuchsia flowers, intense colors that enriched the landscape with vibrant hues.

Next to them, fragrant white jasmines sprouted from the bushes, giving off a sweet, enveloping scent. The jasmines were flanked by the rose plants, which opened in shades of red, pink, and white.

Rosa then stopped to observe a plant that grew abundantly in the wild and in the form of an evergreen bush, Emily looked at it reminded him of normal rosemary, but with a different flower that turned into a wonderful triumph of blue flowers, the girl compared them' to many precious lapis lazuli set in the green and rock. For this reason she explained to him that Rosa was one of the most famous plants of the island, its name was "Blue of Capri", all this she told him while picking some bunches to decorate, together with other flowers, the tables of the restaurant.

As they walked along, they were inundated with the scent of citrus fruits, and Emily was stunned by the sight of rows and rows of lemon and orange trees.

Rosa approached a plant full of large lemons and explained to Emily that "citrus fruits were probably introduced to Capri in the 10th century and have characterized the colors and scents of the island's air ever since. Lemons, which began as an ornamental plant, were soon used for the goodness of the juice and the properties of the essential oils extracted from the peel. World famous is the lemon liqueur "Limoncello", to be enjoyed frozen. The Capri lemon, called "femminiello", has an elongated elliptical shape and is medium to large in size. It first bears fruit in October, with the juiciest fruit of the year; in March the light yellow lemons, called "bianchetti", ripen; and in June the "verdelli", the green ones. Emily picked one that was yellow with a very thick peel, its scent was intense, she loved lemons and even limoncello, she admitted to getting a little red in the face.

As they walked along, they were inundated with the scent of citrus fruits, and Emily was stunned by the sight of rows and rows of lemon and orange trees.

Rosa approached a plant full of large lemons and explained to Emily that "citrus fruits were probably introduced to Capri in the 10th century and have characterized the colors and scents of the island's air ever since. Lemons, which began as an ornamental plant, were soon used for the goodness of the juice and the properties of the essential oils extracted from the peel. World famous is the lemon liqueur "Limoncello", to be enjoyed frozen. The Capri lemon, called "femminiello", has an elongated elliptical shape and is medium to large in size. It first bears fruit in October, with the juiciest fruit of the year; in March the light yellow lemons, called "bianchetti", ripen; and in June the "verdelli", the green ones. Emily picked one that was yellow with a very thick peel, its scent was intense, she loved lemons and even limoncello, she admitted to getting a little red in the face.

CHAPTER 7

At the restaurant, Emily was flanked by a girl from Capri named Aurora. She was a young woman with long brown hair framing a delicate face, with lively, smiling eyes of a beautiful hazel color, always elegant and well-groomed in her attire, wearing fashionable clothes and always impeccable, a sunny and sociable girl with an affable personality that impressed everyone she came in contact with.

Then there was the cook, a young man also from Capri named Marco. He was a tall, athletic young man with short dark hair and expressive green eyes that caught the attention of everyone who looked at them. Marco was a very charming young man with a strong presence and a smile that won the hearts of many girls. He usually wore a simple t-shirt and jeans, but managed to make them look fashionable and cool with his charismatic personality.

Both Aurora and Marco, who worked with Emily at Gaetano and Rosa's restaurant, were very professional and passionate about their work. Aurora was an attentive and caring waitress, always ready to advise customers on the best dishes on the menu and make sure they had a memorable dining experience. Marco worked in the kitchen as an assistant chef, demonstrating his culinary skills and, under Gaetano's watchful eye, inventing new dishes that were a feast for the senses.

Rosa was an excellent hostess and mentor to Aurora, with an innate grace in the way she got things done, a reassuring presence to her employees who genuinely cared about their well-being and success.

From the first meeting, Emily had a feeling that she would get along well with both of them. Aurora had been very understanding and patient in explaining everything to her, even giving her tips on how to set up tables and clean up faster.

With Marco she had not had a chance to talk yet, they had introduced themselves very quickly and in that moment he had explained to her the order of the orders and where to put the dirty dishes, only that, but a few times she had caught him watching her from his station in the kitchen, while he was talking to Rosa or arranging the flowers on the tables or when he was helping Aurora to clean up.

The girl found him very charming, he had a very sensual smile.

During the first few days of work, Emily flanked Aurora a little, and Rosa helped her with English for orders.

He noticed that the people all arrived at the same time - it was unbelievable - it was as if the customers had an internal clock that chimed at the same time.

As time went by, he began to learn the dishes and how to bring them to the tables, clearing and tidying up quickly, as sometimes there was a line of people waiting outside the restaurant.

The day passed quickly, and when the last of the customers were gone. She literally collapsed in her chair, her feet aching.

Aurora looked at her and smiled and patted her on the head, saying, "You'll see, you'll get used to it, it's just a matter of time," then sitting down next to her as she dried some cutlery, she confessed to her, "I remember the first days I worked here, I used to come home that I was beat, But I liked and still like working here, even after some years that I did it," then turning to look at Rosa and Gaetano standing in the kitchen, he said with tears in his eyes, "Gaetano and Rosa are my family here, we all feel like family, if someone has a problem, Gaetano and Rosa go out of their way to solve it. "Then she took a handkerchief and dried her tears. "I was welcomed here when I got pregnant six years ago, my family did not accept that I was unmarried, so I came here to ask for a job and Rosa, who knew my situation, helped me and hired me, I stayed in the apartment where you live now, then after Giorgio, my son, was born, I got married to my boyfriend, I bought a house, but I will never forget what they did for me ..Rosa is a special woman with a big heart. Remember that."

Emily turned around, her face moved by what she had just heard, and looked at Rosa who was helping Gaetano tidy up the kitchen, the woman who might have been staring at you lifted her eyes and met the girl's, her look so sweet and maternal filled Emily's heart who excitedly looked away.

They finished ordering, then a devastated Emily said goodbye to everyone and returned to her apartment.

She entered, turned on the small lamps that were placed in the corners of the room, took off her shoes and found that they hurt a lot, it was as if she had a thousand needles under the soles of her feet, slowly she walked to the bathroom. She ran the hot water to take a warm bath.

She walked to the kitchen and realized that she had not bought anything, she desperately opened the refrigerator and magically saw that someone had filled it with fruits, vegetables and some dishes ready to heat. She could not believe her eyes and realized that it was Rosa, she had surely entered the apartment when she left with Gaetano and had put some supplies and some leftovers from the kitchen in it.

She was hungry as hell, she took a hermetically sealed container, she opened it and found cold pasta with mozzarella, basil and cherry tomatoes in it, she took a fork and went to the hall, there was a small balcony where a tiny round table and two chairs were placed, she sat down and looked at the illuminated coast and a full moon reflecting its rays on the calm sea, she enjoyed her first meal alone in the company of "only" a beautiful moon and the wonderful sea of Capri.

CHAPTER 8

The guttural cries of seagulls woke Emily, who was sleeping peacefully in her bed.

The window, left open the night before, let in the rays of the rising sun.

The sea air was fresh and Emily, still asleep, staggered to the small balcony, where the sight was incredible. From a distant balcony overlooking the sea, Emily floated with a bright and alert gaze. Her eyes were enraptured by the magnificent spectacle before her. A gentle breeze caressed her hair, and the salty scent of the sea breeze filled her nostrils, immersing her in a sense of serenity and well-being. The waves of the sea danced in a hypnotic symphony, gently caressing the shore, their foaming chimes. Emily watched in wonder as the golden reflections created a path of brilliant light on the water, as if the sun itself had poured into the sea, giving the landscape an enchanted aura.

Beyond the horizon, the outline of Capri emerges from the shadows of the night, revealing its timeless beauty. White houses with colorful roofs overlook the sea, creating a picturesque image, gracefully perched on the cliffs like a perfect postcard.

Seagulls broke the morning silence with their guttural cries, adding a joyous note to this symphonic scene. Emily felt the beating of her heart in sync with the rhythm of nature, as if it were an integral part of everything around her. Slowly, the sun rose higher in the sky as the Sea of Capri turned into a dense carpet of silver, radiating an enchanting glow. Emily knew that this fleeting moment was a gift reserved for a select few, a testament to timeless beauty that her soul welcomed with awe and serenity.

From this balcony overlooking the sea of Capri, Emily felt blessed to be present in this moment of purity and wonder. The sunrise she had watched so delicately had awakened in her a feeling of gratitude for the enchanting beauty that enveloped this little corner of the world.

Inspired by the energy that nature had given her, she decided to go for a run, and after a quick breakfast of orange juice and a rice galette, she put on her running suit and shoes, and with her iPod, set off on her adventure.

He quickly ran down the narrow street that led to the sea and came to a square where there was a large fountain with a statue.

From there, he decided to take a path paved with stones that led to the sea.

The surrounding vegetation consisted of bougainvillea, aromatic plants and lemon trees that framed this beautiful path. For Emily, it felt like flying.

Suddenly she saw a house surrounded by greenery, in front of her an open white wooden gate, Emily noticed that there was not a soul there, she decided to go inside to have a closer look, and still running, she ran down the driveway that led to the building, which was lined with lemon and orange trees, the smell was intense.

After a few minutes of running, Emily found herself at the entrance to the mansion.

It appeared to the girl to be unoccupied. Emily stopped and watched.

She sat down on one of the three steps leading to the front door and stood still, listening to the silence and admiring the sea that could be seen. This house was the home of Emily's dreams.

A gentle breeze caressed her face and the sound of crickets accompanied her thoughts.

Who knows whose house this is?

She offered to ask Gaetano about it, then intrigued, she got up to inspect the land around the house and was surprised to see that nearby was an immense piece of land with many rows of vineyards.

Emily walked among the rows of vines. She wondered if this vineyard could produce good grapes and thus good wine. To diagnose whether a vineyard was in good condition, Emily knew that you had to look at the foliage of the plant to see if it was being fed and to be sure that the vines were in good condition.

By looking at some of the leaves, he was certain that the vineyard was in good condition.

Emily would have liked to stay a little longer, but looking at the clock she realized it was time to return, shower and get ready for the restaurant.

Reluctantly, she walked back up the driveway, but turned around and admired the little house surrounded by greenery once again, closing the gate and smiling as she made her way back, her mind and heart enraptured by this place that seemed magical to her.

CHAPTER 9

"Did you sleep well Emily?" Rosa asked as she saw her enter the restaurant, all smiles, happy with the run she had just made, she replied, "Yes Rosa, I slept like a log, I want to thank you for filling my fridge, you were very kind and I really appreciated the pasta you left me, I ate it all last night," Rosa said as she rearranged the kitchen cupboard, "You have to thank Marco for that, it was his idea," Emily looked at Marco in surprise, who was cutting some vegetables in the meantime, the girl smiled a little embarrassed and approached the boy, looking at him she said, "Thank you Marco for your kindness," he looked up with his big green eyes and with an intense look that stopped the girl's heart he replied, "You're welcome, I thought you might be hungry . Anyway, anything, just ask," he smiled.

"My goodness, what a stunner you are." He thought and looked at the vegetables he was chopping and could only say "Thank you Marco".

Together with Rosa they set up the tables for the reservations they had for lunch, then Gaetano' called her to show him what they were cooking.

On the fire were two large copper pots of fish with cherry tomatoes, basil and potatoes.

Emily approached the pot and smelled the aroma it gave off - it was delicious.

Marco watched with a satisfied smile the countless expressions on Emily's face, which were true manifestations of what she was feeling and experiencing, and in that moment he understood that this girl possessed a sweet and innocent soul like that of a child, with a great enthusiasm for all new things. He liked this American girl with big black eyes and long wavy hair and a slim but strong body.

"Gaetano, I wanted to talk to you about something," the girl asked, tasting a piece of bread with fish sauce that Marco offered him.

"Tell me about it, Emily," Gaetano asked as he sat down in a chair, "while I was jogging I saw a house that looked unoccupied," explaining the way he had run so that he would know which house he was talking about.

"Do you know who the owner is?" Gaetano looked up from the pot and with an amused face turned to Marco who was standing behind him and raised the ladle towards the boy, "You'll have to ask Marco if he owns that house."

Emily's eyes widened in surprise and she stared at Marco who stopped chopping vegetables and looked at her and said, "Yes Emily, the house belonged to my grandmother who left us a few months ago, now it's closed because' I haven't had time to decide what to do yet, unfortunately with work," she shrugged and made a guilty face.

Felicity said enthusiastically, "It's beautiful, the gate was open and I went in, it has a huge piece of land, in addition to the fruit trees there are countless rows of vineyards, it has won me over, you could have those vines pruned and make great wine," the men looked at her surprised by her authority on the matter, Emily saw their astonished look turn red in her face and lowered her eyes embarrassed, "Well, before I came here I read some books about wines and as for the house I worked for a couple of years in a real estate agency in New York," she said.

While Emily was talking to the two men, Marco's gaze was lost in the emptiness of his mind, thinking back to the house, it had been a long time since he had been there, returning there was still very painful for him, the memories were still vivid and especially the lack of his grandmother was still strong.

When he came to himself and saw Emily's face so enthusiastic, he thought it might be the right time to face his ghosts, so he suggested, "If you want, we can go together after work, what do you say?" Emily got up from her chair with her energetic manner and happily replied, "Yes. I'd like to see you inside. Satisfied, she returned to the room, where some customers were already arriving.

CHAPTER 10

Emily was excited to see again the cottage that had fascinated her so much.

After work, she went to change in her apartment and decided to put on a long white linen dress and a wide-brimmed white panama hat, put her white loafers on her feet and took the bag she usually carried over her shoulder, inside which she put her cell phone; she planned to take many pictures.

She was coming down the stairs when she saw Marco waiting for her with his red Vespa parked in front of the door. The boy greeted her with a smile and complimented her on her choice of clothes.

Without wasting any time, Emily jumped into the saddle behind Marco and held on tight. With a roar of the engine, they set off and quickly found themselves riding through the narrow streets. Emily clung even tighter to her riding companion. She felt the cool breeze on her face and the excitement spreading through her entire body.

Along the way, Marco led Emily through the picturesque streets of the city, past the main monuments and down hidden lanes known only to the locals. Every so often, they would stop to admire the view or take a short break, and Emily would take the opportunity to snap a few photos to capture the moment.

They finally arrived at Marco's house. The beautiful house was surrounded by a lush garden with many lemon and orange trees that greeted them and accompanied the couple down the driveway that led to the house. Emily got off the Vespa and looked around in amazement, once again appreciating the great silence and peace that surrounded this property.

In front of the house, a lush garden stretched down to the street. Colorful flowers and aromatic plants grew in abundance, creating an explosion of color and fragrance. A stone path lined with climbing roses led to the entrance of the cottage.

Rows and rows of vineyards stretched behind the cottage. The vines, laden with ripe bunches of grapes, stretched as far as the eye could see, creating a green carpet that merged with the horizon. The scent of ripe grapes mingled with the earth and mown grass, creating an aroma reminiscent of the harvests of yesteryear.

Marco took the keys from a jar near the entrance and confessed to Emily, "My grandmother always had so much faith in her neighbor and left the keys here for everyone to use, but I must say that no thief ever showed up.

The door opened with some difficulty and Marco went to open the windows to let in light and air.

Opening the large windows magically revealed the great room with a large fireplace, all the couches and furniture were covered with a sheet to protect them from dust, Marco and Emily removed these sheets and a large cloud of dust invaded the room. The boys laughed, then with agility Marco walked into the long hallway that led to the sleeping area, there were three bedrooms and two bathrooms.

The kitchen was adjacent to the hall on the right, large windows allowed sunlight to gently filter in, creating a pleasant and inviting lighting. The floors were made of dark wood, giving the room a warm touch.

The furniture was antique, and even the stove was vintage in style. The walls were painted a soft yellow, creating a sophisticated and cozy atmosphere. An elegant marble counter ran along the wall, providing space for food preparation and a quick lunch area.

Exposed shelving above the counter displayed colorful ceramic plates and decorative dishes, adding a splash of color and personality to the kitchen. A large solid wood dining table occupied the center of the room, surrounded by comfortable upholstered chairs. Passing through the kitchen, one entered a veranda from which one could enjoy a panoramic view of the vineyards. A comfortable set of outdoor furniture was placed on this porch, where one could relax and enjoy al fresco meals on sunny days

Surrounding the land of the vines was an expanse of lush green where the vines stood in neat rows. The land looked as if it had not been cultivated for a long time. Mark saw all this and was bitter about it, and as he tried to remove the weeds that had grown around the rows of vines, he said, "I thought Paul, my grandmother's helper, came here to keep the house in order, but as I see I was wrong," and with a gesture of anger he threw them to the ground, Emily approached him and stroked his arm, saying in a sweet tone, "Marco, you could not have known that you are always busy in the restaurant, I can understand that it is painful for you to come here," Marco looked at her and realized that she was right, he could not blame himself completely, but now that he saw the house again, he felt an urge within himself to start something new, to experience something new.

Suddenly he began to run through the rows and he saw himself small again, when in the summer he stayed in that house with his beloved grandmother, running he remembered when to play a trick on him he hid, grandmother would look for him and not finding him she would call him to come out because lunch was ready.

So many memories...

Mark remembered those moments of his childhood, a few tears wet his face, those tears of sadness in reliving those moments as a child together with his grandmother, moments now long gone and unrepeatable, but which now lived in his heart like small treasures to be defended from time.

After exploring the house, Emily and Marco lay down in the garden under a large lemon tree.

Emily looked through the thick intertwined branches of the tree , the blue sky with its white clouds, clinging to the branches were endless lemons, she observed them were a strong yellow color like the sun, she reached up and took one and smelled its strong fragrance then took a bite of that ripe fruit.

Marco looked at her, she was just a beautiful girl, full of life, he had never met such a girl ,always with a smile and those big eyes full of light and happiness.

She thought back to when she had first entered the restaurant with her backpack and that lost but confident look of someone who expected so much from life, full of trust in others and fate.

"You really like lemons, don't you?" Emily smiled and said with her mouth full, "Yes, very much, and then here with this sun they taste different from the ones we get in New York, they are much sweeter and the peel tastes different, they are much juicier."

They stood there talking, then Marco looked at his watch and said, "Quick Emily, we have to go back to the restaurant."

Emily jumped back on Marco's Vespa, and on the ride home they laughed and joked about some outrageous things that had happened at the restaurant.

CHAPTER 11

Marco, in addition to being a beautiful boy, had a sweet and sensitive soul, he was born on this island and loved it with all his heart, he could not imagine living anywhere else, he had everything he needed, he had moved away from Capri just to study in a cooking school.

There he had learned the techniques to become a good chef, his dream was to be able to get a Michelin star, it was a desire he had in his heart since childhood when he had begun to love cooking with his grandmother, from her he had learned many tricks that he now used in his dishes.

The kitchen was his favorite place, next to fishing.

An only child, his mother was from Milan, she had landed on the island to be a teacher and met his father, a well-known policeman, they fell in love at first sight, they married, they had stayed permanently in that corner of paradise where time seems not to pass and it is always summer.

Marco was born in Ferragosto, his mother said that he had never felt so hot as on that day the thermometer reached 42 degrees. When he was born they called his father who was in the barracks, he came running dressed in his military uniform, he wanted to go to the delivery room at all costs, the doctors had to hold him by force to dissuade him.

When she heard the sound of her son's first cry, she finally calmed down and happily made the sign of the cross, knelt down and said some prayers to thank the good Lord that everything had gone well.

They let him into the room and gave him the little creature in his arms wrapped in a green cloth, and as he looked at it, he realized that it would be his second great love in life, after his wife. The child, who understood what his father was feeling, gave him a big smile and the sky opened up for this man and a ray of sunlight enveloped them.

The mother had wanted a baby for a long time, but it didn't seem to be coming, and then she and her mother-in-law had started making novenas to all the saints in heaven, and finally someone up there heard their prayers, and one winter night she became pregnant.

Marco thought about all these things as he prepared some dishes in the restaurant; the visit to his grandmother's house had excited him more than he thought.

The walk down memory lane had shaken him.

Their parents had been in Milan for a few months now, after the death of their grandmother they had decided to make a change of scenery, it was painful for them to stay there as well.

Marco had had a few love affairs in his life, but always with tourists who spent the summer on the island, fleeting stories without consequences, so every summer he had a different love and in winter he remained alone.

The mother was not very happy with her son's behavior, she would have liked to see him settle down with a nice girl, there were several girls on the island who would have done anything to be with him, but he had nothing but work on his mind.

As he was soaking a fresh octopus in hot water, he looked up to the room and saw Emily with her big smile talking to a couple of Americans and something changed in his heart, he stood with the fish in his hand and was deeply absorbed in observing Emily, Gaetano saw him standing there motionless with the octopus in his hand and the pot of hot water and followed his gaze, where his eyes were enchanted and he understood, he smiled under his mustache and approached him saying "the octopus is waiting Marco," he woke up as if from a deep sleep, threw the fish into the pot and turning red with embarrassment, lowered his gaze and resumed his work.

Gaetano was a very private man, and he had said nothing to anyone about this incident, but as the evening went on, thinking back to Marco staring at Emily with the octopus in his hand, he smiled at the idea that perhaps Marco, the great conqueror of female tourists,

had fallen in love!

CHAPTER 12

Emily was very energetic that evening, she felt good, she was happy, she had spent a nice afternoon with Marco, this house had won her over, she kept thinking about this beautiful abode.

Occasionally, while he was working in the dining room, he would look into the kitchen and see the two cooks very absorbed in their work.

He liked Marco a lot, he was nice as well as a handsome guy, it was very inspiring to talk to him, during the motorcycle ride the boy explained to him some tricks for cooking some culinary dishes from Capri.

Sometimes she would meet his gaze and an emotion would invade her...

When the last customer had left, Aurora said goodbye to everyone and walked out of the restaurant where her husband had come to pick her up, Emily watched her walk away with her husband, the two of them holding hands as the full moon illuminated the narrow road leading to the village.

She greeted everyone and went up to her apartment, turning on the lamps scattered in the corners of the room and laying down on the sofa, she was tired.

She closed her eyes. Then someone knocked on the door she got up with difficulty ,opened the door and found herself in front of Marco who with an embarrassed smile was holding a bottle of sparkling wine and two glasses, , and asked "Would you like to have a drink together tonight I would like to make a toast to my grandmother .today was the first time I came back to her house and so many emotions filled my heart, thanks to you I had the courage to face my ghosts" Emily smiled happily and let him in and they sat at the small table on the small balcony and looking at the full moon, whose rays reflected on the calm sea creating silver trails, the two boys toasted to Marco's grandmother whose name was Grace and admiring this unique and unrepeatable scenery they began to know each other a little better..

CHAPTER 13

"Hi Emily, how are you? Terry wants to say hi!" Susan's voice could be heard loud and clear from the computer screen, Emily smiled happily as she saw both her friend and the muzzle of her little dog licking the screen...seeing this scene, the girls laughed.

"When are you coming?" Susan replied, "I asked for an early vacation, they have to give me an answer these days, if they give me the okay Terry and I will pack up and come."

Emily was pleased.

She would have liked to tell him about the lovely evening she had spent with Marco the night before, but she decided to do it when he saw her in person.

The days passed quietly and Emily made many friends, especially with an English couple who had a beautiful house overlooking the sea, in front of which Emily passed almost every morning when she went running. The couple greeted her from the terrace, and once they sent her to visit their house, and she was impressed.

In fact, the English gentleman, now retired, had been the owner of one of London's most famous galleries, and together with his wife, a beautiful woman with long silver hair that she wore gathered in multicolored headbands, they had decided to move to this island and take their furniture and paintings with them.

The house was a renovated rustic, had a huge patio with a beautiful front garden from which there was a spectacular view of the sea.

They had been regulars at the restaurant for several years, arriving at the same time on Sundays in their white Spider convertible, and Rosa always reserved the same table for them. They always took some appetizers, then Gaetano went to their table to greet them and recommend some new dish or the catch of the day.

They always had the same house white wine and a bottle of sparkling water.

They were always very elegant in their linen suits, he always wore his Panama hat and his pipe in his jacket pocket, which could not be absent from his attire, even in the summer when it was very hot, they were there with their smile and their elegance, which also gave luster to the place

Emily adored them, seeing them come in was like stepping back in time, their demeanor so aristocratic and refined.

They always left excellent tips, which Emily shared with Aurora.

The English couple, whose names were Alfred and Mary, had a great affection for this girl named Emily, who would rush by every morning; just seeing her made their mornings brighter, thanks to the beautiful smile and great energy the girl exuded just by talking to them or perhaps entertaining them for a few minutes.

In fact, a few times the girl would see them at the gate of the villa, stop to chat with them and then greet them as she continued through the narrow streets of the island, they would follow her with their eyes and, happy to have seen her, return to the kitchen for their English breakfast.

This morning habit made the couple feel less lonely.

They had never had children, and they saw in the American girl with the big smile a daughter they never had.

Some evenings, when the restaurant was closed, they would invite her to dinner and spend delightful evenings talking about London and New York-two metropolises so different, yet so fascinating.

"Emily, would you like some more cake? "Mary asked him as they sat on the terrace and had just finished dinner.

Emily, slumbering with a sense of peace, looked at the lady and smilingly replied, "No, thank you, Mary, as usual, you cooked divinely and the roast beef was really outstanding." Alfred looked at his wife and saw her smiling smugly at this compliment, he knew his wife adored this girl and his appreciation made her happy.

Alfred asked, "Has your friend been on vacation?" as he lit his pipe with great elegance.

Emily made a sad grimace and replied, "No Alfred, unfortunately there is a lot of work and they didn't give permission, I miss my dog, I hope they can join me next month."

Alfred frowned, sorry to see Emily so sad about missing her pet.

He sighed deeply, admired the sea and said, "Work!!! I have spent my life devoting every moment of my life to work. It is not worth it. Yes, it gives you satisfaction, power and money, but then you get to my age and think you could have worked less and enjoyed life more. Fortunately, I had my Mary by my side, who, despite my frequent absences, remained faithful to me," he said, looking with love-filled eyes at the woman by his side, who returned his gaze and, smiling happily at his words, replied, "Yes, Alfred, I stayed by your side because I loved you and I still love you as I did on the first day," Emily, hearing these words, felt a chill and thought that they were an exceptional couple, perhaps one of the few she knew who still loved each other so much after so many years of marriage.

"What about you, Emily, when are you going to devote some of your time to love?" she looked at Mary who was watching her with a mischievous smile, the girl turned to Alfred and he was also staring at her with the same look. Embarrassed, she lowered her eyes and took the glass of water to drink, taking her time to think of the best answer.

"I don't know," the couple laughed as they saw the poor girl's expression, "but Emily you already have a possible love in front of your eyes!" Said Mary loudly, the girl turned her head and asked with a questioning look, "Mary, excuse me, but what do you mean?" Mary walked over to her with her chair, took his hand between hers and whispered, "When we come to the restaurant on Sundays we can't help but notice that Marco is attracted to you, we watch him and from the kitchen he doesn't stop looking at you, he watches you in everything you do" Emily's mouth opened slightly as if she was about to say something but the words didn't come out. Her face was a perfect picture of astonishment and disbelief. "She couldn't understand. Mary saw that the girl had not honestly noticed anything and asked, "But how could you not notice?" The girl nodded her head and remained silent. Alfred intervened, "Emily, it often happens that you don't notice that there is someone next to you who is attracted to you.

It happened to me with Mary, it was a mutual friend who told me that Mary was interested in me and I saw her every day at the university."

Emily was silent for a moment, the words seemed to hang in the air. Her eyes widened slightly, a light of surprise shone in them. Then, slowly, a shy smile formed on her lips. It was not a broad smile, but rather an expression of gentle wonder, as if she was trying to comprehend the scope of what she had been told. Her cheeks blushed slightly and she lowered her eyes, almost as if she were embarrassed. But when she raised her eyes again, there was a light of hope in them, a glow that was not there before.

After a few moments of silence, Emily said in a low voice, "I met his gaze a few times, but I didn't think he was interested in me."

"Well, from his behavior, we think so,you should investigate,you would make a really good couple." Emily, although the patio was lit only by a few candles, you could clearly see that her cheeks had turned bright red, the English couple looked at each other thinking they had hit the jackpot, but out of politeness they said nothing.

Emily returned home, Mary and Alfred's words still echoing in her mind. "Marco might be interested in you." She sat down on the sofa, her heart pounding in her chest. She hadn't noticed, or maybe she didn't want to. After the last disappointment, the idea of falling in love again seemed too painful.

She looked out of the window, the starry sky, countless stars filled the celestial vault, it was a beautiful night, she frowned and wondered 'why didn't I notice? But deep inside she knew the answer. She was afraid. Afraid to open her heart again, afraid to get hurt.

But now, with the possibility that Marco might have feelings for her, she felt a glimmer of hope. Maybe it was time to face her fears. Maybe it was time to give love another chance.

She thought it was just a good friendship, like the night he had come with the bottle of wine, she had experienced it as something friendly, but maybe thinking about it now and remembering his movements and his looks, maybe it could be that he was interested in her....

She had been from the first moment she had seen him, but after the last affair she had promised herself not to manifest her feelings anymore, rather to nip them in the bud, so that the feeling she had felt had suffocated her, she had promised herself in her heart not to think about love, but now she felt that everything was changing. Now the games were open between her and Marco, the game had begun and the whistle had been blown by Mary and Alfred.

CHAPTER 14

The next morning she slept longer than she should have, she had thought a lot about her life and understood how fear had taken over.

"Emily come I need you," Rosa's voice echoed from the courtyard, Emily looked out the window and saw the woman greeting her, the girl signaled that she would come down quickly.

"Hi Emily, I need you to help Marco in the kitchen, Gaetano has a fever today," Emily's eyes went wide and she thought, "Oh God in the kitchen?" Rosa sensed her thoughts and saw the look of panic on her face and reassured her, "Emily, don't be afraid, Marco will tell you what to do, rest assured! And they walked at a fast pace towards the restaurant.

Inside, Aurora was already setting up a table with twelve covers, and other tables were already ready; many people had made reservations for lunch that day, but in the evening, Rosa had decided that the restaurant would be closed and had canceled the reservations.

Panicked, Emily looked through the large kitchen window and saw Marco busy cleaning some fish. "Go ahead, Marco will tell you what to do," Rosa told her as she pushed her towards the kitchen, Emily entered the kitchen with an unsteady step, the boy looking at her pointed to some vegetables in the wooden crates to be washed and cut, Emily happy with the task assigned to her began to work. In her mind she thought, "Well, cleaning vegetables is not difficult and then I saw Gaetano how to do it," and singing under her breath she began to help.

Marco was very upset, it was the first time he had everything on his shoulders, since he had been working there Gaetano had never been absent, he must have been very sick to do this.

He had many thoughts and worries in his mind but decided that he had to prove to himself and Gaetano that he could run the kitchen alone, then he looked up as Emily, singing under her breath, was washing the vegetables, looking at her his face lit up as if he had just seen the sun after a long night. Her eyes, full of admiration and affection, shone like two stars in the night sky. Her lips curved into a sweet and sincere smile that revealed her inner joy. Her cheeks were colored with a light blush, a sign of her deep love. His gaze was full of tenderness and devotion, as if enchanted by the beauty of his beloved. It was as if everything else in the world had disappeared, and all that remained was her.

Then he tried to concentrate on the work at hand.

The first customers arrived and the first orders came into the kitchen, the chef had assigned Emily her tasks and the girl was ready.

The initial anxiety Marco had felt suddenly vanished.

Marco moved through the kitchen with a grace and precision that was almost hypnotic. Despite the pressure, there was no trace of panic or haste in his movements. Every gesture was calculated, every action precise.

His hands danced on the stove, stirring, slicing, seasoning with a rhythm that was almost musical. Although he was alone in the kitchen, he seemed to be in control.

Emily looked at him admiringly. Even though Gaetano was sick and the restaurant was full of customers, Marco did not seem worried at all. In fact, he seemed to be enjoying every moment.

His passion for cooking was evident in every dish he prepared. Each plate was a work of art, a tribute to his skill and love of food.

Despite the pressure, Marco remained calm and focused. With a smile on his face and a twinkle in his eye, he continued to cook, proving to everyone that he was a true master in the kitchen.

Emily contributed to the good work they were doing, they were very coordinated in the action and Rosa, looking from the arch that separated the kitchen from the dining room, was thrilled with the way things were going, the dishes coming out were perfect and in her heart she thought that maybe they were even better than her husband's, but she kept that in her heart.

Emily was fast, under Marco's orders they looked like a team that had worked together for years.

Aurora listened to the compliments of many diners as she brought the dishes to them, and some noticed that some of the dishes had something new and appreciated it. After the last customer had left, the two boys in the kitchen looked at each other contentedly, Marco sat down to rest while Emily put the last dishes in the big dishwasher and then sat down next to him, tired.

Finally there was silence in the room and in the kitchen. They stayed like that for a few moments, then Emily looked up admiringly with her big black eyes and exclaimed, "Marco, you were phenomenal, everything went perfectly, the dishes came back empty, everyone liked it, you really are a great cook.

Marco looked at the girl, his eyes shining with appreciation and a sincere smile forming on his lips."Thank you, Emily," he said in a tone that revealed his gratitude. His gaze lingered on her, as if he wanted to capture and preserve this moment in his memory. It was a moment of pure connection, a moment that spoke more than a thousand words.

Marco stood up and took Emily's hand to get her up and confessed to him, "Anyway, it was a team effort and to thank you, since the restaurant is closed tonight and we didn't have time for lunch, I want to invite you to a picnic at my grandmother's house, would you like to? Let's take some things from here and relax under a lemon tree that you love, what do you think, assistant chef?"

Emily smiled happily and replied jumping for joy, "Yes chef I also gladly accept because' I'm hungry!!!" and they both laughed.

Rosa watched them from the room and felt a thrill in her heart, she was happy to see these two boys together, they formed a beautiful couple and smugly finished setting up the room.

Emily and Marco climbed onto the Vespa, the engine humming quietly as they prepared to leave. The streets of Capri were a maze of twists and turns, but Marco knew them very well.

The wind blew through their hair as they drove, the sun shone high in the blue sky. The scent of flowers and the sea filled the air, a sweet melody that only Capri could offer.

They arrived at Marco's grandmother's house, a white house with blue shutters and a lush garden awaited them, a place that exuded a feeling of serenity and love, a place Marco called home.

They prepared the picnic in the garden, under the shade of a large lemon tree, a perfect time to enjoy each other's company.

As they sat down to eat, Marco looked at Emily with a smile. Thank you for being here,' he said, his voice full of gratitude. Emily replied with a smile, happy to share this moment with him. They ate in the silence that this place exuded, both feeling good, looking into each other's eyes and happily tasting the food that Marco had prepared with his own hands and that both seemed even more delicious.

Marco had also brought an excellent fresh white wine that they tasted with beautiful goblets that they took from Grandma's kitchen and sat on a colorful carpet to enjoy their first picnic together.

As the sun went down, Marco looked at Emily. The golden light of the sunset illuminated her face, making her even more beautiful. He could not take his eyes off her. He watched her as she laughed, as she talked, as she ate. Every gesture, every expression, every word made her more fascinating in his eyes.

He felt an impulse, a desire so strong that he could no longer ignore it. He wanted to kiss her because he loved her.

So he approached her, his heart pounding in his chest, he said in a low voice, "Emily can I...can I kiss you?

Emily looked at him surprised. But then slowly she nodded. "Yes, Marco," she replied with a shy smile.

And so, under the starry Capri sky, Marco kissed Emily. It was a sweet and passionate kiss, a kiss that spoke more than a thousand words. A kiss that expressed all the love, all the desire, all the passion he felt for her.

Emily responded to the kiss with the same intensity. She felt a feeling of warmth spread through her chest, a feeling she had never felt before. It was as if everything else in the world had disappeared, leaving only the two of them.

When they parted, they looked into each other's eyes. There were no words to say, only smiles to exchange. They both knew that that kiss had changed everything. They knew that from that moment on, nothing would ever be the same again.

They returned that by now it was dark, Emily was enraptured by that kiss from Marco, she had felt an emotion she had never felt before as if all the loves she had experienced up to that moment were just a bad copy of the one she felt now She got off the Vespa and Marco walked her to the door of her apartment, she opened the door and staying at the entrance gave him another kiss then he caressed her and whispered in her ear saying "Good night Emily. Sweet dreams," and went down the stairs. Emily followed him with her gaze as he rode away on his motorcycle and from that moment she knew that she had fallen madly in love with him, that she was madly in love with this boy with the sensual smile and who could kiss beautifully...she raised her eyelashes and went singing back to her apartment.

CHAPTER 15

Emily arrived at the restaurant early and saw Marco singing as he arranged the fruit and vegetables that had just arrived. She spotted Beppe waving at her from his yellow truck and then hurried away.

Upon entering, Emily met the gaze of Aurora, who observed her with a smile and walked over, taking her under her arm and asking, "Do you want to tell me what you did to that poor boy? He came earlier than usual, he's in a great mood and kind to everyone, and he sings."

Emily blushed and lowered her eyes; she did not speak, but Aurora understood that something had happened between them.

"Emily, can you come to the kitchen for a moment?" Marco's voice interrupted that awkward moment, especially for Emily, who was glad she did not have to answer and ran into the kitchen.

Marco smiled at her with a big smile on his face and handed her a plate to taste, Emily took her fork and tasted. Marco had prepared a dish that looked like something out of a starred restaurant in Capri. In the center of the plate was a freshly caught fillet of sea bream, grilled to perfection, its juicy white flesh falling off at the touch of the fork. The fish was lying on a bed of creamy lemon risotto, the grains of which had absorbed the fresh, citrusy flavor of Capri lemons, creating a perfect balance with the sweetness of the bream. All around, a sprinkling of fresh parsley added a touch of green and freshness. The dish was completed with a drizzle of extra virgin olive oil, which added an extra layer of flavor and a slight sheen. It was a dish that pleased not only the palate but also the eyes.

Emily took a bite of the new dish Marco had prepared. Her eyes immediately lit up. It was an explosion of flavors in her mouth, each ingredient blending perfectly with the other. She could not hold back a sigh of joy. This is so good!" she exclaimed, looking at Marco with an appreciative smile. "I have never tasted anything so delicious."

"Emily," said Marco, looking into her eyes with a serious expression. "I dedicate this dish to you." Her words were full of emotion. "It is you who inspired me to cook it, to create it. Last night, after our picnic, I came home and was so excited that I locked myself in the kitchen and started experimenting with new flavors until I came up with this culinary composition, and as I was cooking it I was thinking of you. Your laugh, your smile, the light in your eyes. And I tried to capture some of that light in this work I created.

Emily was speechless for a moment, then a sweet smile lit up her face. "Thank you, Marco," she replied, her voice full of gratitude and affection. "I can't think of a better compliment." And they kissed softly.

As Marco and Emily lost themselves in a passionate kiss, Aurora and Rosa watched them from the restaurant room. Their eyes were wide with surprise, their mouths open. They had not expected this development. They watched the scene with a mixture of astonishment and curiosity, wondering if this would mean a change

for the future of the two boys, but also for the future of the restaurant?

CHAPTER 16

"Emily, they gave me vacation time!!!" Sarah's voice echoed in the room, the girls were on video call, Terry barked as if to warn her mistress that she would soon join them.

Emily's eyes widened in surprise and she let out a cry of joy, "Yay finally!!! I can't wait to see you!"

"Let me know when you have the plane" "Sure," replied the friend, "I'm going to go to the travel agency I have downstairs now and we'll take the first flight to Italy......"

After talking to her friend Emily went out onto her small terrace; she had just finished work, Gaetano was back at full speed at work, and Marco had resumed his job as a cook's helper.

Soon Marco would arrive to pick her up , they would take a Vespa ride; he wanted to take her for a drink at a seaside bar.

"A sky ready for a beautiful sunset accompanied Emily and Marco as they ventured into a picturesque café in Capri. The scent of the sea mixed with the aroma of fresh coffee from the café created an almost magical atmosphere. Seated at a small table outside, they could hear the gentle sound of waves crashing on the shore and the distant echo of Italian music.

Marco ordered two glasses of limoncello, Capri's famous liqueur. While they waited, they were lost in thought. When the waiter arrived with their drinks, the crystal glasses reflected the light of the impending sunset, making the limoncello seem even more golden.

They laughed and toasted their adventure, their eyes shining with happiness. That evening in Capri, amid laughter, shared stories, and the sweet taste of limoncello, Emily and Marco would create memories they would cherish forever.

"Emily," Marco began, in a somewhat uncertain voice, "there is something I want to talk to you about." He paused, searching for the right words. "You know, the experience I had in the restaurant, when I was alone, shaped me. It made me realize that I can make a quantum leap, I studied to become a chef but in those years I didn't have the chance to really express my work, at the restaurant I'm very good, with Gaetano and Rosa they are special people, but now it's time for a change, I want to be the one to decide what to cook and how." "In his eyes, Emily saw the passion and fire burning in him, that fire that makes you make decisions and turns in your life that will change you forever."

The girl's eyes were filled with curiosity as she watched him. "What do you mean?" she asked.

Marco took a deep breath. "I want to open my own restaurant. A place where I can express my creativity, where I can share my passion for cooking with others."

Emily was silent for a moment, surprised by Marco's confession. Then a smile appeared on her face. "That's a wonderful idea, Marco," she said. "It would be a big step, but I believe in you. You are a great cook."

Marco looked relieved. "Thank you, Emily," he said. "But... I could use your help. Are you willing to help me?"

Emily nodded, her smile widening. "Of course, Marco. It will be a pleasure to help you make your dream come true."

And so they began to plan their new adventure together.

"Do you have any idea where you want to open your restaurant? " the girl asked, Marco looked at her fondly and gave her a light kiss, then I took his hand and whispered, "In my grandmother's house! Emily widened her eyes and smiled broadly, "Great idea Marco, it is a perfect place, I am one hundred percent with you!

And then they ordered another limoncello and made a toast, Marco raised his glass and said, "To our future" Emily was struck by those words and an immense emotion came over her, maybe she had found her future in him?

"Would you like to go for a ride? It's still early," Emily drank and got up from her chair, "Sure Commander, I'm at your disposal," Marco hugged her and they ran to the Wasp.

As they walked among the vineyards, Marco and Emily began to imagine what their restaurant would look like. They thought about how they could use fresh ingredients from the garden and orchard, how they could create a menu that reflected tradition and innovation. Grandma's cottage, with its rustic charm and idyllic location, seemed like the perfect place to realize their dream.

"Imagine," Marco said, "we could serve our dishes under these trees, overlooking the vineyards. And we could use the grapes to make our wine."

Emily nodded and smiled at the idea. "That would be wonderful," she replied. "And I'm sure we can do it."

And so, as the sun set and the stars began to shine in the sky, Mark and Emily continued to dream and plan, excited about the adventure ahead.

Emily and Marco stood in the cottage, surrounded by the tranquility of nature. The glittering flames of the fireplace illuminated the room, creating an intimate and cozy atmosphere. They exchanged a glance, their eyes filled with desire and passion.

They slowly approached each other, feeling the warmth of each other's bodies, their hands intertwined in a tender gesture of affection as they lost themselves in passionate kisses that followed each other with increasing intensity. The caresses became deeper and more sensual, exploring the contours of their bodies as they joined in a passionate embrace.

Their breaths mingled in a synchronized rhythm as they surrendered to the present moment. The soft music playing in the background enhanced their emotional connection, making the experience even more intense and magical.

In that moment, in the cottage shrouded in the silence of the night, Emily and Marco were lost in each other, swept away by a wave of pleasure and happiness. Nothing seemed to matter but their love for each other, eternal and unmistakable.

As night fell on the cottage, Emily and Marco stood there, wrapped in each other's arms, dreaming of the future they would build together. It was a perfect moment, one they would remember forever.

CHAPTER 17

Marco's father was a rugged man with gray hair and piercing eyes, a policeman born and raised in Capri. He had an air of authority that was reflected in his confident manner and deep voice. Despite his profession, which gave him many responsibilities, he had a kind and affectionate side, especially when he spoke of Capri, his birthplace.

Marco's mother, an elegant and refined woman, a teacher from Milan. She had a warm, inviting smile and eyes full of wisdom. A woman of great culture and intelligence, she had instilled in Marco a love of learning.

One day they invited Emily to lunch at their quintessential Capri home. The house was a charming white building with blue shutters, surrounded by a lush garden full of colorful flowers and lemon trees. Inside, the decor was simple but cozy, with wooden furniture and whitewashed walls.

Lunch was served on a large wooden table in the garden, under the shade of a wisteria-covered pergola. On the table were platters of fresh fish, tomato and mozzarella salads, and, of course, bottles of homemade limoncello.

As they ate and laughed under the Capri sun, Emily felt welcome and at ease. It was as if she had become part of the family. And in that moment, she realized how close Marco was to his parents and his homeland.

As they ate lunch in the shade of the pergola, Marco's father turned to Emily. "Emily, you told us you were from New York. What is life like there?" he asked, his voice calm and interested.

Emily smiled as she remembered her hometown. "New York is an amazing place," she replied. "It is full of energy and life. Every day is different and there is always something new to discover. But I have to admit that Capri has a charm all of its own."

Marco's mother nodded, her eyes full of understanding. "I understand," she said. "Milan has its own rhythm too, but Capri... Capri has a different soul. It is a place where one can find peace."

Lunch continued with light chatter and laughter. Emily talked about her adventures in New York, the lights of Times Square and the charms of Central Park. Marco's parents listened with interest, asking questions and sharing their Capri stories.

Despite the cultural differences, there was a sense of mutual understanding and respect. Emily felt welcome and valued.

After lunch, Marco took Emily by the hand and they left the house, hopped on his ubiquitous Vespa, and set off to explore some wild places.

CHAPTER 18

The boat with Sarah aboard slowly approached the picturesque harbor of Capri. The afternoon sun reflected off the crystal clear water, creating a play of lights that danced on the ship's hull. Sarah, with Emily's faithful dog on a leash, looked out from the bulwark and watched the island come closer and closer.

On the pier, Emily waited impatiently. The sea breeze ruffled her hair as her eyes scanned the horizon for the first sign of the boat. As soon as she saw it, a smile lit up her face. She couldn't wait to hug her friend and her beloved dog again.

When the boat docked, Sarah got off first, and Emily's dog ran happily toward her mistress. Emily greeted Sarah with a warm hug, happy to see her old friend again after so long. Laughter filled the air as the two women chatted.

They took a typical Capri taxi and all were happy on their way to the restaurant and their apartment,

On the way, Sarah admired the island, enraptured by its colors, scents, and such quaint houses, and looked at Emily and told her it was an incredible sight.

They arrived at the restaurant, then together they went upstairs to the apartment, upon entering Sarah was speechless, "But it's beautiful Emily, it feels like being on a ship, all this nautical style decor is perfect," then she looked out onto the small terrace and took a long breath of sea air, the sun was high in the sky and from that position you could admire the sea that looked like a blue table that day.Terry ran all over the apartment, then tiredly she sat down on the sofa and fell asleep, Emily looked at her lovingly Sarah came back from the kitchen, sat down and said, "We are a little tired, Terry and I, the trip was long." Emily accompanied her to the bedroom, "We will have to share the bed, I have made room for you to put your things in there, there are towels in the bathroom if you want to freshen up.

Now I have to go down to the restaurant if you are hungry, there are some very tasty leftovers" Sarah opened her eyes amazed by these words and ran to the kitchen, opened the refrigerator and replied happily "Well, we are not going to starve, go easy, now we will rest " Actually Terry on the couch was already in the dream world and soon Sarah would join her.

CHAPTER 19

"Sarah meet Rosa and Gaetano" Emily's friend came to visit her friend after a few hours.

As she entered the restaurant, she was thrilled to see the decor and especially the food being brought to the tables. Sarah greeted her with a smile and introduced herself "Good evening I'm Sarah Emily's friend" she managed to say in Italian with an American accent, Emily looked at her in surprise and asked "Sarah but where did you learn Italian?" she replied with a smug smile "After you left I took an online course I didn't want to come here and not understand anything..." everyone laughed and the owner sat them down at a table for two and said "Sarah now I'll get you something to eat".

Marco watched from his seat, curious about her, Emily talked about her a lot.

Sarah looked towards the kitchen and met Marco's eyes and he waved at her, her friend realized who it was so she waved back.

Emily was very busy that evening with a group of Americans who had recently arrived on the island and had decided to taste all the dishes on the menu, Emily and Aurora ran from the kitchen to the large table without taking a breath.

Suddenly Marco from the kitchen had some dishes ready, but the two girls were busy, so spontaneously Sarah, seeing that they were in trouble, got up and went to the kitchen and asked "what are these and where should I put them" Marco looked at her and thanked her and said "at the big table is spaghetti with clams" Sarah with the agility and speed of a New Yorker brought the dishes and asked in their language if they needed anything else. The group, hearing that there was another American in the restaurant, applauded and ordered more bottles of wine.

When he returned, he took the order back to Rosa who was at the cash register, then he went to the bar where Gaetano was and got the bottles of wine he had ordered. Gaetano smiled at her and thanked her for her help. Sarah was happy to help.

The girl worked hard all evening, she also went to the kitchen to rearrange the dishes while Marco and Gaetano were busy cooking, Emily and Aurora never stopped for a moment with the tables and customers.

When everything calmed down, they all found themselves in the kitchen eating a chicken sandwich that Marco had prepared, Gaetano opened a bottle of fine Italian Prosecco for the occasion, and as they uncorked the bottle, they toasted to the newcomer, Sarah, who had been their savior on this very confused evening.

"You know Emily, this is a very special place, you were right. You feel part of something unique and magical, there is so much love around you, Rosa, Gaetano, Aurora and Marco are special people, I enjoyed being able to help out tonight, I felt part of something beautiful," Sarah said as they sat on the small terrace admiring the sea, legs stretched out, drinking a glass of wine, Terry was still sleeping peacefully on the sofa. Emily looked at her friend, who at that moment was staring at the sea and the lights of the coast, and replied, "Yes, Sarah, that's right, here you are not a number, here you are a person, unfortunately New York is a beautiful city, but you can never have the human relationship you can have here. And here I'm fine and maybe I've found my little paradise to live in.

Sarah turned around and said with a surprised look, "Are you going to stay here then?"

"Well, haven't I told you everything? Something good is brewing between me and Marco and I am madly in love with him," Sarah shouted, "Finally! I am happy my friend! That you have finally found someone who loves you, I like Marco so much, I can tell he is a real and sincere person, so let's have a toast to you both," and raising their glasses, they clinked glasses as the moon looked at them with a smile.

CHAPTER 20

They slept soundly until Terry jumped on the bed and woke them up barking, and with great difficulty the two girls got up. Emily turned on the coffee machine and, as she did every morning, went out onto the balcony and stretched, breathing in the salty sea air.

It was a clear day, the sky was cobalt blue, and the clouds, few in the sky, were white and formed funny shapes. "Of course waking up every morning and seeing this view is not for everyone," said Sarah as she came up behind Emily, who smiled and nodded, knowing full well that it was a privilege to be there.

The sound of the coffee machine distracted them from their thoughts and they returned. They had a quick breakfast of coffee, orange juice and rusks, accompanied by a fabulous jam Rosa had made with strawberries, all delicious. Then Emily went downstairs with Terry to show him around and as she was walking she got an idea, she went to the restaurant and there was Gaetano and she asked him if she could take his car for a few hours, he said yes.... Felice went back to the apartment, Sarah was getting dressed and as she walked in she called "Sarah get ready I have a surprise for you!" she looked at her in curiosity, she finished dressing and in a few minutes Sarah, Emily and Terry were ready.

They went down the stairs and headed for the car, Sarah looked at her with a look of fear, "Don't you want me to sit up there?" Emily put Terry in the open space behind her and opened the door for her friend, making a mini bow, "Madam, your carriage is ready," she widened her eyes and nodded no, but then got in at her friend's insistence.

Emily was driving Gaetano's car for the first time, she was not very experienced, in fact sometimes the three-wheeled vehicle made risky braking maneuvers, but after a few minutes her driving became smoother, making the passengers happy and content.

They walked through the narrow streets of Capri, with Sarah sitting beside her.

The Ape, with its humming engine and distinctive shape, moved nimbly through the narrow, winding streets of the island. The white houses with red tile roofs, colorful flowers hanging from the balconies and the scent of the sea mixed with that of lemons created a magical atmosphere. Sarah looked around in admiration, taking in the beauty of the island.

Emily, with a smile on her lips, drove on, happy to have her friend nearby. Eventually Marco's grandmother's cottage appeared, which, with its blue windows and white walls, seemed to be part of the landscape, as if it had grown there naturally.

Emily parked in front of the cottage and helped her friend and Terry down. Together they approached the hut. Sarah, seeing the place for the first time, was speechless. Emily said with a proud smile, "Welcome to our future restaurant." She continued, "Marco and I have a plan. We want to open a restaurant in this cottage. We will start preparations soon."

Sarah listened intently and her eyes lit up at the idea. Working in a marketing firm, she knew how important it was to have a good strategy for a new business. She looked around and saw that from the driveway leading to the house she could see the sea, Emily accompanied her and gave her a tour of the house, including the front where there were endless rows of grapevines. After the tour, they sat under a lemon tree and lay down on the grass and looked up at the sky and said, "Emily, this is a great idea!" "I would love to help you. I can use my marketing skills to get the word out about your restaurant, I have my network of American clients and friends who have cooking columns on national networks that I could contact," Emily hugged her friend happily for her offer. She knew that with Sarah's help, her restaurant would have every chance of success. And so, together, they began to plan the future of their restaurant. And in that moment, they both knew in their hearts that they were embarking on an unforgettable adventure, united by a strong friendship and a desire to change their lives.

CHAPTER 21

That same night, Marco decided to talk to Gaetano.

After the last customer had left the restaurant, Marco approached the man. he took a deep breath, gathered his thoughts, and prepared to say what he had been thinking the past few days.

"Gaetano," Marco began, his voice echoing in the silence of the restaurant. "I have something important to tell you."

Gaetano, who was arranging some bottles of wine on the shelf, turned to look at Marco. "Sure, Marco. Tell me," he replied, putting down the bottle he was holding.

Marco took another breath and said, "I have decided to take a new path, you know that for me cooking is my life and now I feel the time is right to do something truly my own, so it is with much regret and sadness that I inform you that I will be leaving the restaurant. I have decided to open my own restaurant with Emily in Grandma's Cottage.

Gaetano remained silent and in that moment he thought back to when he was very young and came to work with him in his restaurant, in that boy, so sharp and innovative, he saw himself again at his own age. She liked working with him, he was a professional, at that moment, listening to Marco's words, she was not very surprised, she knew that sooner or later he would go his own way and so, with a broken heart, she made an understanding smile and replied, "Marco, you have been a valuable member of our team and I wish you all the best in your new project. I am sure you will do a great job. We will miss you, but I understand. It is right that you go your own way, you are a complete chef, I have taught you all my secrets and you have learned them by adding something of your own and creating new and ingenious dishes, I am sure you will be successful and if you need help I will always be there for you.

Marco was so moved by her words, so fatherly and loving, that he hugged her. Then Gaetano wiped away his tears, patted him on the back and said, "Now come, let's open the best wine and go call everyone, I want to have a little party to celebrate".

Marco ran into the next room where Rosa, Emily, Aurora and Sarah were and told them to join Gaetano, the intrigued women arrived in the restaurant room and saw Gaetano holding his best bottle of wine he owned and said loudly "Tonight our Marco informed me that he is going to open his own restaurant and I want to celebrate his success with you" then with a pop he opened the bottle and everyone applauded, the women looked at each other moved and Emily admired Marco's courage.

After the toast, the boy spoke and thanked Gaetano for his kind words and for all he had learned from working with him. As Marco left the restaurant that night, he knew a new chapter in his life was about to begin. And he couldn't wait to see what the future had in store for him and Emily.

CHAPTER 21

Marco's grandmother's cottage, with its blue windows and rustic charm, was the perfect location for their restaurant. Nestled among lush vineyards, it offered breathtaking views that promised to make every meal an unforgettable experience.

Preparations began in earnest. Marco and Emily, along with their friend Sarah, worked tirelessly to transform the cottage into a cozy restaurant. The days were full of activities: cleaning, painting, installing kitchen equipment and setting up the restaurant.

The blue windows were cleaned until they shone, allowing sunlight to flood the interior of the cottage. The walls were painted a bright white to set off the wooden beams of the ceiling. The furnishings were a mix of modern and rustic, with solid wood chairs and tables that perfectly matched the cottage's atmosphere.

The heart of the restaurant was the kitchen. Marco and Emily installed the new equipment and made sure everything was perfect for food preparation. The oven, stove, refrigerator and dishwasher were carefully placed to create an efficient workflow.

Behind the cottage, the vineyards also offered a spectacular view of the ocean. Outdoor tables and chairs were placed to create an alfresco dining area where guests could enjoy their meals while admiring the view.

Sarah, with her marketing experience, offered valuable advice and helped with key decisions. Even little Terry, Emily's dog, seemed to take part in the preparations, running happily between everyone's legs.

Despite the hard work, the atmosphere was one of excitement and anticipation. Every day, Marco and Emily's dream of opening their restaurant came closer to reality. And with Sarah's help and Terry's company, the journey was as fulfilling as the goal they all had in their hearts.

One day, after a day of hard work setting up the last tables in the garden, Marco, with a heart full of hope, decided to take an important step, took Emily by the hand and led her to the part of the house that was not reserved for the restaurant, and in a sweet and sincere tone, asked Emily, "Would you like to come and live here with me in the cottage?"

The question hung in the air, filling the room with anticipation and hope. Emily looked at Marco, his eyes shining with a special light, that light you have when you realize that your dreams are coming true, that light you have a few times in your life that makes you realize that the future you have always wanted and desired is there, waiting for you with open arms.

Part of the house was dedicated to them, a cozy and comfortable space, perfect for quiet living after long days working in the restaurant.

CHAPTER 22

Gaetano came a few times to see the work and contributed a lot of important advice that the children listened to, Marco did not leave him alone, contacted a chef friend of his who was looking for work and called him, so in a few days he arrived and took his place in Rita and Gaetano's restaurant.

One evening, while they were still at Rosa's apartment, Emily received a call from her parents, they had been informed about the big event of the restaurant opening and Marco, and they were happy for their daughter, her brother heard from him from time to time, he was now in London on business, but promised that as soon as he had a few days off he would join her.

After talking to them, Emily went out onto the small terrace where Sarah was working on the computer, "Look Emily, do you like it?" she said, turning the screen towards her. She couldn't believe her eyes, Sarah had made a website about Marco's restaurant, on the main page there was a beautiful picture of the cottage and the vineyards and the sea view, she had also included Marco's picture with all his credentials and reviews that customers had given him over time when he worked at Gaetano's.

It was stunning, Emily was speechless and looked at her friend with her mouth open in amazement and exclaimed, "I knew you were good but here you have outdone yourself. Sarah blushed a little embarrassed and replied, "It's just the beginning, I have a lot of things in mind and if Marco really wants to experiment with a new cuisine, mixing and combining different Italian flavors and traditions, who knows, maybe one day he won't get his coveted Michelin star?"

Emily jerked up from her chair, excited only by the thought that her beloved Marco might one day be rewarded as he deserved, and gazing fixedly at the sea, she sighed, "Here all wishes can come true.

And suddenly a shooting star was clearly seen above them, lighting up the sky with its trail.

The two friends silently held hands and gazed at the star, each expressing his own wish in his heart.

CHAPTER 23

The opening day of the restaurant had finally arrived. The sun was slowly setting, tinting the sky with pinks and oranges, as the cottage with the blue windows lit up to welcome the first guests.

Emily and Sarah, elegantly dressed, greeted the guests at the entrance. Their faces lit up with excitement and nervousness, but mostly with joy. This was the moment they had waited and worked so hard for for several weeks.

Gaetano arrived with his wife Rosa. They were both visibly proud of Marco and Emily. Gaetano looked around the restaurant, silently approving the changes they had made to the cottage.

Aurora, who had offered to help in the early days of the opening, moved nimbly between tables, serving guests with a smile. Her experience and presence added a professional touch to the event.

The restaurant was filled with laughter, chatter and the clinking of glasses. Guests were enjoying the delicious cuisine prepared by Marco and Emily, praising their skill and the quality of the food.

As the evening wore on, Emily took a moment to look around. She saw the restaurant filled with happy guests, heard the echo of laughter and toasts, and realized that all the effort had been worth it.

During the opening, while the atmosphere was full of celebration and merriment, Sarah found the right moment to talk with Emily. The two friends moved away from the hustle and bustle of the party and retired to a quiet corner of the restaurant.

"Emily," Sarah began, "I have some news for you." Emily looked at her curiously, "I've decided to ask my company to work remotely. That way I can stay here on the island and help you and Marco with the restaurant."

Emily was surprised for a few seconds, then a smile spread across her face. "Sarah, that is wonderful news!" she exclaimed, hugging her friend. "We're so happy to have you here with us."

And so, as the party continues, Emily, Marco, and Sarah toast their future together, excited about the adventures that lie ahead.

Marco had taken as his assistant a fellow student from the hotel school, he was English and specialized in starters and desserts, dishes he did not feel very strong about.

His name was Jeff and he was from London but he had lived in Italy with his family for many years, he was tall with blond hair and two blue eyes, he had the face of a person with a strong and determined character, he and Marco had bonded immediately during the learning period, he had shared the apartment together, both of them helped each other, Marco gave him tips for the first and second courses while Jeff, being a good Englishman who loved sweets, helped him in the preparation of desserts, together they complemented each other.

In the period when Marco was maturing the idea of opening his own restaurant, he had in mind only Jeff as his helper, he had full confidence in him, he knew that he was a professional with a strong character, but also calm, especially under pressure and there, if the work would go as he hoped, there would be a lot of it.

He called him one morning and when Jeff heard that he was opening his own restaurant, without asking him anything, he replied, "Friend, I'll come and help you, give me time to notify the restaurant owner and I'll come to you. I am in Vienna and it is cold, I will gladly return to the Italian sun". And they laughed in his heart, Marco knew he could count on him, he was a true friend.

Marco and Jeff had a truly innovative and original menu, they both wanted a Michelin star and there was a chance to get it.

When Sarah had the final restaurant menu, she immediately posted it on her website and circulated it among her friends in America.

From the first day of opening, reservations started coming in, word was getting out that people were coming from the mainland, and the website and social media were doing a great job of marketing.

Sarah was now staying in a room in the cottage, but wanted to find a small apartment of her own.

Jeff and Sarah decided to look for a place to share together.

One day, they made some appointments with local real estate agents to look at apartments. Marco's red Vespa, parked in front of the restaurant, gleamed in the island sun. Jeff, with his driving experience, casually climbed into the driver's seat while Sarah sat behind him.

They began their journey through the winding streets of Capri, the Vespa humming softly as they moved between the white houses and colorful shops. The sea breeze ruffled their hair as they enjoyed the breathtaking view of the island and the blue sea.

They visited different apartments, each with its own unique charm. Some offered spectacular views of the sea, others were hidden among the cobblestone alleys, each telling a different story. But they were sure they would find the right apartment, a place they could call home while they lived and worked on the island.

After a long day of searching, Jeff and Sarah finally found the perfect place. It was a small apartment on a quiet street in Capri, just steps from the sea.

The apartment was cozy and bright, with white walls and terracotta floors that reflected the sunlight. The entrance opened into a small living room with a comfortable sofa and a bookshelf full of books. Next to the living room was an open kitchen, perfect for preparing home-cooked meals.

The two bedrooms, though small, were cozy with two double beds and a window overlooking a small garden. The bathroom, with its blue and white tiles, was simple but functional.

But what really made this apartment special was the small terrace. With a breathtaking view of the sea and the rooftops of Capri, it was the perfect place to enjoy a cup of coffee in the morning or a glass of wine at sunset.

As they toured the apartment, Jeff and Sarah realized how much harmony there was between them. They shared the same tastes, finished each other's sentences, and laughed at the same things. A complicity was born between them that day, a bond that could become more than just friendship.

The day ended with a spectacular sunset as Jeff and Sarah, tired but happy, rode back to the restaurant on the red Vespa.

Now Sarah, clinging to Jeff's waist, felt an emotion in her heart; she too, like Sarah, had just come out of a very complicated relationship with one of her co-workers.

A story that Sarah was only now calling "sick," he was the classic guy who doesn't want to commit, who promises you but then never keeps his promises and makes up countless excuses.

She had spent two years of her life waiting for the phone to ring, only to find out through a mutual friend that her dear colleague was engaged to the boss's daughter.

At that moment, he understood why he had run away in the middle of the night after spending the night with her. The canceled appointments and Christmases spent alone waiting for him, at that moment he understood that she had been a fool.

Surely, he had gotten engaged to the boss's daughter just to get to the top of the company and nothing else, such a man did not know how to love, he only loved himself.

CHAPTER 24

Emily got out of bed one morning to find that she was alone. Marco had left a note on the kitchen table informing her that he and Jeff had gone to the harbor to pick up the day's catch, and that they would meet later. Next to the note was a tray of breakfast. Happy Emily stretched like a cat in her pajamas, opened the large window, and sat on the outdoor sofa she had inherited from her grandmother while she ate her breakfast, admiring the early morning sunlight,

Suddenly she had the mad urge to write down the feelings she was feeling at that moment, so she went back inside, took her notebook and began to write. The pen moved fast and without noticing she had written many pages, she was excited, she reread what she had written and an emotion invaded her.After a long time the desire to write had returned. She was happy, she got up from the chair and started dancing, Terry who was next to her jumped for joy imitating her mistress.

Then, calming down, he sat back down and looking over the papers, he heard a voice inside... whispering, "Emily, write the novel of your life."

Raising her eyelashes in surprise, she realized that she could tell everything she experienced, she did not have to make up stories. She had a chance to put her past and present experiences on paper, and perhaps it was time for her to return to her passion, writing.

When Marco returned, he was presented with "a scene he never imagined he would see, Emily was sitting on the floor writing in a notebook and had dozens of papers scattered around her on the floor, Terry saw him coming and ran up to greet him, while the girl, so engrossed in writing, did not even notice his arrival.

Marco was surprised, remained silent and watched her for a few minutes, then he sat down next to her, came up with his face and gave him a kiss on the cheek', Emily only noticed his arrival at that moment and looked at him, hugged him and stood up' she said excitedly.

"Dear, I've started writing again, I'm super happy, I can't stop myself, the ideas come like rivers in flood, the emotions are translated into words quickly and easily. Now I will start and finish the novel I have always wanted to compose, now I feel that here with you on this island I will be able to compose a work full of love and passion. And she stood up and spun around, her long hair flying and her movements sweet and melodious like a ballet dancer, Terry and Marco watched her twirl and stood in silence admiring this angel moving through the air.

CHAPTER 25

Sarah worked remotely for his New York office and went in the evenings to help out at the restaurant, a very nice love affair had developed between her and Jeff, they understood each other instantly, had the same tastes and loved the desserts he made for her in their small kitchen overlooking the sea.

The restaurant was now famous, many celebrities who were on vacation on the island would go there to dine, and this was the greatest publicity one could have, because' all these celebrities were followed by a flock of paparazzi, who in their articles, in addition to talking about the VIPs, mentioned Marco's restaurant as a popular destination.

Marco was happy with his work, but he always wondered if he would ever have the chance and the joy to receive his Michelin star.

One day, a distinguished man entered Marco's restaurant. Although he presented himself as an ordinary customer, there was something in his demeanor that suggested he was no ordinary visitor, but an inspector for the Michelin Guide, known for his reserve and refined palate.

The inspector sat at a reserved table, carefully observing his surroundings. His gaze took in everything from the restaurant's cozy atmosphere, to the neat decor, to the attention to detail, and he noted it all in a small booklet he kept hidden on the table.

Marco, aware of the importance of this visit, made sure that everything was perfect. Every dish that came out of the kitchen was a masterpiece, both in taste and presentation. The inspector tasted each dish carefully, taking his time to appreciate each ingredient and the skill with which it was prepared.

Despite the tension, service continued smoothly. The restaurant's professional and courteous staff moved gracefully between tables, ensuring that every customer, including the inspector, received impeccable service.

The Michelin inspector's visit was a significant event for Marco's restaurant. It was recognition of the hard work and passion that Marco and his team put into creating an exceptional dining experience. After the inspector left, leaving behind an air of expectation, Marco knew he had given it his all. Now all he could do was wait.

A few days passed with no news, Emily finished her book, Jeff and Marco continued to experiment with new dishes even as they wondered if they had gotten the star they so longed for.

One night, just as the restaurant was about to open to the public, the phone rang and Emily went to answer it.

Marco and Jeff were in the kitchen preparing food, suddenly a scream came from the room, Marco and Jeff came out of the kitchen in a panic to see what had happened and saw Emily standing on a table looking at the two chefs who were there watching her petrified, she raised her arms in victory and shouted "We have our Michelin Star".

There was silence as everyone looked at Emily, then she repeated, "We have our Michelin star. "Jeff and Marco looked at each other and squealed with joy and hugged each other, then Marco grabbed Emily who had remained on the table and kissed her while Jeff hugged Sarah who had remained motionless at the news.

Happiness was in the air. It was a night of celebration, after work everyone went to the beach and bathed in the moonlight, lighting fires and singing at the top of their lungs the songs they loved most.

Suddenly Marco looked into Emily's eyes and confessed, "I could not have done it without you, from the first moment I saw you with your backpack on your shoulders and your bright smile, I knew that with you I could climb the highest mountains in the world. You are my star, my inspiration, the air I breathe. I bless the day you entered my life. I love you."

Emily upon hearing these words began to cry and hugged him and repeated, "I love you too."

Emily finished her novel, which was a hit, quickly becoming a bestseller, and needless to say, she never left the island again; it became her home.

Sarah stayed on the island, although sometimes she and Jeff would return to New York for work or to feel the excitement of the big city, but after a few weeks she would return to her small apartment near the sea.

Rosa and Gaetano decided it was time to retire, so they closed their restaurant and traveled the world.

Tom and his wife Maria decided to spend the winter months in Capri, while Emily and Marco enjoyed the summer months in New York.

The British couple had lunch in their restaurant every Sunday, as is their tradition, happy to have contributed to the love between Marco and Emily.

What else to say? Ah, Emily's colleagues are still there with their submissive gaze in their meeting room, looking at the gray sky and the skyscrapers. Hoping that something will change in their lives.

They do not know that only they can change their lives, with courage and strength like our protagonist Emily.

Armed only with her audacity, her unfailing smile. With her backpack on her shoulders she crossed the Ocean and with determination and positivity she changed her life.

I wish this to all dreamers and lovers of freedom....

BUENA VIDA A TODOS...

(I look forward to your reviews and opinions.

Follow me on my blog selvaggiastark.blogspot.com

to be informed about my upcoming releases ...)

Made in the USA
Columbia, SC
22 June 2024

37369433R00089